Lee McClain

S ZZLE

A NOVEL

MARSHALL CAVENDISH

Front cover original photo © shutterstock.com/ Valeriy Lebedev

Other Marshall Cavendish Offices: Marshall Cavendish International (Asia) Private Limited,
1 New Industrial Road, Singapore 536196 • Marshall Cavendish International (Thailand)
Co Ltd. 253 Asoke, 12th Flr, Sukhumvit 21 Road, Klongtoey Nua, Wattana, Bangkok 10110,
Thailand • Marshall Cavendish (Malaysia) Sdn Bhd, Times Subang, Lot 46, Subang Hi-Tech
Industrial Park, Batu Tiga, 40000 Shah Alam, Selangor Darul Ehsan, Malaysia

Marshall Cavendish is a trademark of Times Publishing Limited

Library of Congress Cataloging-in-Publication Data
McClain, Lee.
Sizzle / by Lee McClain.
p. cm.
Summary: When the aunt she lives with becomes ill, orphaned Linda Delgado must leave
Arizona for Pittsburgh, where she struggles to adapt to a huge foster family, eating canned
food, and finding an outlet for her love of cooking.
ISBN 978-0-7614-5981-1 (hardcover) — ISBN 978-0-7614-6093-0 (ebook)
[1. Family life—Pennsylvania—Fiction. 2. Cooking—Fiction. 3. Moving, Household—Fiction.
4. Foster home care—Fiction. 5. Mexican Americans—Fiction. 6. Orphans—Fiction. 7.
Pittsburgh (Pa.)—Fiction.] I. Title.
PZ7.M47841366Siz 2011
[Fic]—dc22
2011001234

Book design by Becky Terhune
Editor: Marilyn Brigham

Printed in China (E)
10 9 8 7 6 5 4 3 2 1

ᴍᴄ Marshall Cavendish

*To my sister, Sue Spore—
my first and best cooking partner*

I would like to thank my student Nicole Taft for writing the poem "O Romeo" specifically for Chloe; my agent, Steven Chudney, for urging me through multiple drafts of this and other projects; and my editor, Marilyn Brigham, for seeing the strengths of the manuscript and adding to them. Here in the Pittsburgh area, I learned so much from my friends in the Tuesday morning writing group: Sally Alexander, Betty Howard, Karen Williams, Kathy Ayres, Dick and Pat Easton, and Colleen McKenna. And most of all, I'm grateful to my family, Mike and Grace, who put up with more than their share of cooking from cans while I worked on this book.

Chapter One

I'm not bragging when I tell you that I have the best nose in all of Arizona.

I don't mean it's extra beautiful or anything. The most anyone would ever call me—let alone my nose—is cute.

But my sense of smell is so good that I can tell exactly which type of peppers are in any given dish of salsa. Whenever Aunt Elba and I eat something *fantástico* at somebody else's house, I can recognize the spices and re-create the exact same dish at home. One night there was a gas leak in our restaurant, next door to our trailer, and the smell woke me out of a sound sleep.

The downside is that I can tell who hasn't taken a shower, who's been branding cattle, and who's eaten too much garlic three days ago. And if somebody's wearing extra cologne to impress a first date? It knocks me flat.

Top two requirements in a boyfriend, if I ever get one: do take showers, don't wear cologne.

My nose is just one reason I'd rather cook than waitress.

Back in the kitchen, we control the smells. Out front, you're at the mercy of the customer—not that we have as many of those as we used to.

The other reason is the way some guys treat waitresses. If one more customer calls me a hot tamale, I'll explode!

So when Aunt Elba told me I couldn't sleep over at my best friend's house one Friday night because she needed me at the restaurant, I'll admit it: I whined. "I *hate* waitressing."

"Darla's not coming in anymore, remember?" she said, handing me a knife and chopping board. "And Juan needed off. It's just you and me tonight."

"I'm only fourteen. Aren't there laws about forcing me to work?"

"Linda! I let Darla go so I could buy you school clothes. Now get to work." She handed me a huge bag of onions to chop.

Okay, I might have cried a little, but who would know whether it was from the onion fumes or from my life? It wasn't that I wanted to be like the kids on TV, with a mom and a dad and money and no need to work. I loved living here in the southern Arizona desert with all of my aunt's attention to myself; and most of all, I loved cooking fresh, delicious Mexican food in our tiny restaurant.

But Aunt Elba was getting crankier by the day because the restaurant wasn't doing too well. Fewer people wanted to drive the extra ten miles down our lonely stretch of highway for authentic Mexican food. No, they stayed up in Tucson and went to the new Tacos & Toppings chain restaurant.

Not only that but Aunt Elba hadn't been feeling well lately. She didn't complain, but she kept pressing her hand to the side of her head like it hurt; and the bags under her eyes were getting worse.

Thinking about it made me feel bad that we'd argued. I

wiped my eyes on the back of my wrist and looked over at her. She had on rubber gloves to chop and seed the jalapeños for salsa. Taking the harder job for herself, like always. "I'm sorry, Aunt Elba," I said.

"It's okay, *cara mia*." Aunt Elba smiled at me.

"Hey, anybody working here?" called someone from the dining room. And just like that, we were into the dinner hour.

Friday was our busiest night; that was when a lot of men finished a week of work and drove back to family in Mexico, stopping for our all-you-can-eat specials on the way. They kept me hopping with requests for more burritos and enchiladas, and with banging down their Coke glasses and asking for beer, which we didn't even serve. A few guys came in already drunk. Those were the ones to watch out for.

"Hey, little seniorita," one of them called to me. "You got a date for tonight?"

"I got a date with your dirty dishes," I said, struggling with a heavy tray of them.

"Let me take you away from all this," joked another, who I'd known since forever. He weighed about three hundred pounds.

"In your dreams, Robert," I said.

"They bother you too much, you tell me," said a guy named Peter. I sort of knew him because he'd just graduated high school and he had a brother my age. He was really nice. Good-looking. And he smelled great!

"They're bothering me too much," I admitted as I shoved the tray through the pass-through. "I hate waitressing."

He didn't ask me why I did it. He knew we owned the place. "I could take you out somewhere nice when you get off," he said. "Help take your mind off things."

He looked at me as if he liked me—a practically-grown-up man! A funny feeling twisted my insides. "I'm not allowed to date yet," I told him.

"It wouldn't be a date," he said, smiling at me. "How about an ice cream and a drive?"

Without my brain's advice, my body took a step closer to his table. "I'll ask my aunt."

"Just come," he urged me.

"Well—"

A bony hand came down on my shoulder. "She's not going out with you." It was Aunt Elba, pulling me back so she could stand between us, a frying pan in her hand. "This girl is fourteen. She's a child!"

"I'm not a child," I said.

"Kids like ice cream," Peter said.

"No way, forget it. Get outta my restaurant." Aunt Elba lifted the frying pan like she was going to smack it down on Peter's head.

Peter held up his hands in the air and sidled toward the door.

"Aunt Elba," I moaned. "You're totally embarrassing me!"

"You can't afford to be kicking out good customers just because they're nice to your kid," Peter called back over his shoulder. Then he was gone.

Everyone was staring and commenting, and I wished I could disappear. I opened my mouth to complain, looked up at Aunt Elba—and stopped.

Her face was pale, her eyes wide and scared. The frying pan clattered to the floor as she raised both hands to her head. "I don't feel so well," she said, and sank down into the booth where Peter had been sitting.

"What's wrong?" I jumped up and felt her clammy cheek. "Hey, does anyone know what I should do here? She's sick!"

Aunt Elba waved her hand like I shouldn't call attention, but she wasn't able to talk.

One of the guys came over and looked at her. "Can we get an ambulance out this way?"

"Faster to drive her up to the emergency room in my truck," Robert said.

Two minutes later we were on the road, Aunt Elba strapped in between us, gasping for breath.

Chapter Two

Luckily, it wasn't a heart attack or anything like that. The doctors said Aunt Elba was suffering from anxiety. Anxiety, and bad jalapeños.

So forever after, I can say that my life was changed by bad jalapeños.

When we got home from the hospital, Aunt Elba was supposed to rest, and at first she did. We put an ON VACATION! BACK IN ONE WEEK! sign on the restaurant door, and she stayed in bed. I cooked her chicken tortilla soup and watched a lot of TV.

By the end of the week, Aunt Elba was feeling better. Better enough that she said I could invite my best friend, Julia, over for a night of cooking. We did this every couple of weeks, and it was so much fun. Sometimes Julia taught us how to cook stuff she'd learned from her old grandma on the reservation: fry bread or cactus salad or corn salsa. Other times we just tried new recipes from the Food Channel.

That night Julia was begging for chimichangas, which she'd

had at Tacos & Toppings. "They were sooooo good, Miss Elba, but I bet yours would be even better." We were all three standing in the small kitchen of our trailer.

Aunt Elba made as if to swat Julia on the side of the head. "That flattery might work with your mama, but not with me," she said.

Julia rolled her eyes. "Nothing works with my mama. She's too busy with the twins to cook anything but frozen lasagna."

Aunt Elba and I both wrinkled our noses at the same time. We're not big on frozen food around here.

"These chimichangas, they are not real Mexican food," Aunt Elba said. I could tell that the mention of frozen lasagna had weakened her, though. She felt sorry for anyone who had to eat bad food.

"But you know how to make them," I said. "Remember those chicken ones, for Juan's kids? And Rosita ate vegetables without knowing it?"

"Come on, cook with us," Julia begged. "Show us. Please?"

Sometimes I got jealous because of how much Julia loved to cook with Aunt Elba. I'd try to hurry Julia off to my room so we could gossip and listen to music without my aunt overseeing everything.

But Julia loved all the attention Aunt Elba was willing to give us. And since she'd gotten sick, I had an extra appreciation for my aunt, too.

Plus, she'd been acting a little weird this week. She kept putting her arm around me, and patting my head, and touching my cheek—lovey-dovey stuff that wasn't like her. She'd even given me a pair of her grandmother's silver earrings, saying I was old enough to have some family heirlooms, and showing me how to use cactus juice to keep off the tarnish. And once I'd caught her holding a photograph of me as a baby, just staring at it, a million miles away.

It was all very strange, and it made me worried about her. So I wasn't in my usual hurry to escape to my room. "Come on, let's make them," I coaxed.

"What does it mean, anyway, *chimichanga*?" Julia asked. She was smart that way: she loved words.

Aunt Elba and I looked at each other, and my aunt shrugged. "I do not know how to say it in English," she said.

"Something like *thingamajig*?" I guessed.

"All right, all right, we will make these thingamajigs," said Aunt Elba. "*Cara*, what do you want for the filling?" She stood behind me and brushed back my hair with her fingers.

I leaned into her. "Beef and cheese."

She kissed the top of my head. "Beef and cheese it is. Run and get them from the restaurant, and I will chop some peppers."

Julia came with me. "Is she okay? She seems different."

"Yeah, weirdly affectionate, right? She's been like that since she came home from the hospital," I said.

Back in the trailer, we shredded beef and grated cheese and played the radio. While we cooked, Julia and I talked about what was going on in school, keeping it squeaky-clean for Aunt Elba.

Of course, she read between the lines when Julia started talking about a boy she liked. "Those young men will soon grow up enough to bother you," she said. "Keep with your studies and stay away from them. There is time for boys later."

"Oh, Aunt Elba," I said. "That's no fun."

"No fun is taking care of a screaming baby when you're still a teenager," she said. "That's where all this hootchy-kooch with boys can lead."

Julia and I couldn't even look at each other or we'd start laughing. *Hootchy-kooch?*

As we mixed the filling, I got an inspiration. "Let's put in some chocolate and cinnamon, and they'll be, like, *mole* chimichangas."

Julia made a face. "Ugh."

I looked at Aunt Elba. "Don't you think it would be good?"

"Well . . . try a sprinkle of cinnamon, but no chocolate, I think."

So we mixed in the spice, and heated the tortillas, and brushed on egg whites, and spooned in the faintly cinnamon-flavored meat filling. Aunt Elba showed us how to fold them up right.

"Fry them fold side down," she said. "Now, I am going to sit and write this recipe for you girls."

She sounded a little out of breath.

"You don't have to write it down," I said. "Why don't you go rest, and I'll bring you a plate when we're done?"

"No. I must write you copies of the recipe," she said, and sat down at the kitchen table. "*Mi abuela* wrote down her recipes for me, and I will write down mine for you."

"Okay, if you want to." I reached for the oil canister.

"Not too much oil," she said. "That is how Tacos & Toppings does it—deep-fry—but that is not the only way. Just a couple of tablespoons of oil in a cast-iron pan works better. Then we bake."

While the chimichangas were baking, we sat down at the table with Aunt Elba. She'd written out the recipe for Julia, and now she was writing out a copy for me.

"You should see her grandma's recipes," I said to Julia. "They're written on, like, parchment or something, in this gorgeous handwriting. All in Spanish."

Being the geeky girl and good friend that she was, Julia asked to see them, so I brought over Aunt Elba's wooden recipe box and we pulled them out. Not only was the handwriting beautiful, but Aunt Elba's *abuela* had drawn pictures to illustrate some of the steps. These were true keepsakes.

There were recipes for cake, and empanadas, and special

breads for Easter. "What are all the hearts and flowers for?" Julia asked, pointing to an especially decorated page.

Aunt Elba looked over, peering through her Walmart reading glasses. She read the accompanying words, written in such fancy cursive that I couldn't decipher it myself. "Cook with love for best result," she translated, smiling.

"That's so sweet. Hey, what are these recipes?" Julia pulled out a couple of recipes stuffed into the back of the box, written in a different handwriting without illustrations.

Aunt Elba looked and scowled. "*Mi madre*," she said. "Recipes for cheap, bad food."

I knew a little about my mean-spirited grandparents, who still lived in South Texas, though we never saw them. "Why'd you save these, Aunt Elba?"

She shrugged. "It's good to remember. Family is important."

Julia snapped her fingers. "You know what I'm going to do? I'm going to start a foods page in my online community. Or maybe there's an online community for foods. That's how our generation will keep up the traditions."

"On the computer?" Aunt Elba waved her hand dismissively. "Food isn't about computers. Food you need to taste and smell and touch."

"But we watch the Food Channel," I reminded her as I opened the oven door to check on the chimis.

"Why didn't you ever get married, Miss Elba?" Julia asked her. Clearly she was still thinking about boys, particularly Victor Gonzalez.

Aunt Elba laughed. "I am too much the *jefe*. No man wants to come home to that each night." She got up from the table, steadied herself with her hands, and went to check on the chimichangas herself.

"She means she's bossy," I translated for Julia. "And she's

right. She won't let me do half the stuff the other kids at school do."

Julia rolled her eyes. "Don't complain to me. You're the princess around here."

Had she lost her mind? "We're poor," I protested. "I have to work in the restaurant every day. I'm hardly a princess."

"Yeah," Julia said, "but you're the center of her universe."

Later, as I bit into a steaming chimichanga, I realized Julia had a point. Aunt Elba did pay me a lot more attention than Julia's mom paid her. And although Aunt Elba worked me pretty hard in the restaurant, she also made sure I had time to do my homework and see my friends. She almost never bought new clothes for herself, but she would hunt the bargain racks for hours to find me the same kind of outfits other kids wore.

Yes, I was lucky to have Aunt Elba. And after her dramatic trip to the hospital, I was even more aware of it. I never wanted anything to change.

But, like the song Aunt Elba had crooned to me since I was a little girl, you can't always get what you want.

FABFOODZ.COM

Julia Payette

CLICK FOR MORE PICTURES

RELATIONSHIP STATUS:
Single

INTERESTS: Reading, computers, cooking. (Yeah, I'm a geek.)

What I'm cooking today:
Chimichangas

What else I'm doing: Learning to make a FabFoodz page!

Friends/Family/Foodie Comments:

Linda says: Good start, Julia! Tried to get Aunt Elba to post but . . .

Julia says: Yay! I want comments! Where RU?

Linda says: At the library. She thinks it's pamema moderna.

Julia says: Huh?

Linda says: Newfangled nonsense.

Julia says: She'll let you make a page of your own though, right?

Linda says: Yeah. Show me how during study period?

FABFOODZ.COM

Linda Delgado

<u>CLICK</u> FOR MORE PICTURES

RELATIONSHIP STATUS:

Single

INTERESTS: Food, friends, more food, fun!

What I'm cooking today: Whatever our customers order

What else I'm doing: Math and science homework, ugh!

Friends/Family/Foodie Comments:

Julia says: Cute pic! Dreaming of someone special?

Linda says: No! I'm not the boy-crazy one. Hey, we've got to post some recipes on here!

Julia says: How about those, idk, little nutty cookies your aunt makes?

Chapter Three

When I got home from school a few days later, I found Aunt Elba in the restaurant, packing salt and pepper shakers and Tabasco bottles into boxes.

"What are you doing?" I asked.

"Cleaning up," she said. She put more table toppings into her box and wiped down a table with a bleachy rag. "And packing."

"But why?" I threw my backpack on the counter.

She moved to another table. "We're closing down."

"No!" I reached out to stop her from putting away a ketchup bottle.

Aunt Elba draped an arm around me. "Linda, Linda," she said. "I put on some coffee. Let us get a cup and sit."

Something about the way she said it made me feel like clapping my hands over my ears. I had a really, really bad feeling. I sank down into a booth and watched, nervous, while she poured us two coffees and sat across from me.

She looked at me for a minute like she wasn't sure how to begin. Deep creases stood between her eyebrows.

"Just tell me," I finally said.

She reached over, grasped my hand, and took a deep breath. "You know I am not well," she said.

My stomach clenched. "They said it was stress. Only stress."

"Stress made my hypertension worse, that's right."

"And this place stresses you out." I sipped my coffee. I didn't really like its bitter taste, but I liked feeling older.

She nodded, took a breath like she wanted to say more, then stopped.

I looked around. I loved the restaurant, and I'd grown up here. But lately the place had been stressing me out, too. I felt lighter just thinking we wouldn't have to cope with all of the problems. "What are we going to do, though? For money?"

She held up a hand. "There's something else, Linda. I got more test results back today."

I stared at the red splotches that were blossoming on her neck. I was scared to look into her eyes.

"Now they think I had a ministroke."

"What's that?" My voice sounded so calm. A direct contrast to the way my gut seemed to be flipping and my heart pounding.

She waved her hand. "It means I could have a bigger stroke, and I should have some procedure for my hard arteries, and all kinds of things. But I don't want to talk about my health. I want to talk about you."

"I don't—"

"It's time to face reality."

The way she said it drew my eyes to her face. "What?"

"I've been thinking for a while that . . . you need more."

"More what? Money?"

"More than I can give you," she said.

That made no sense. I cocked my head to one side and studied her. Her expression was sad, but her shoulders were squared up straight, as if she was holding herself to very good posture. More red splotches covered her neck.

"This life has been hard on you," she went on, squeezing my hand. "Working all the time, the truckers, not being able to go with your friends—"

"I'm fine, I'm great." I clattered my cup down into my saucer. "I'm not going to live with Grandma and Grandpa. You promised Mom. And they wouldn't take in a *bastarda* like me, anyway, right?"

"*Ssh.* I would never do that to you." She took a deep breath. "But . . . you're pretty. And you're growing up. The *muchachos* aren't going to leave you alone, and I—"

"I'm not even interested in boys!" It wasn't exactly true; I'd started looking, but I had sense. I wasn't going to do anything to get myself in trouble.

She continued as if I hadn't interrupted. "I did see this coming. A year ago, I got in touch with your aunt Pat."

"The *Cooking from Cans* lady?"

Aunt Elba nodded.

I made a face. She was hardly my aunt. This woman, Pat, was the sister of a man who'd married Aunt Elba's cousin. A couple of years ago, she'd learned that we had a restaurant and had sent Aunt Elba a DVD with some episodes from her local cooking show. What a joke.

Aunt Elba wasn't laughing now. "She's willing to take you in."

My breath whooshed out, and I stared at her.

Aunt Elba reached for my hand and squeezed it. "You need a family to help you through the teenage years."

"But . . . *you're* my family." I wanted to say more, but my throat closed up. Aunt Elba had raised me since my mom died when I was a tiny baby. She was the only family I'd ever known, and I'd always taken for granted that she was committed to me. "I can't believe you'd just throw me away."

"My love." She came around the table, wrapped her arms around me, and pulled my head against her chest. "This is the hardest thing I have ever done, but it is the best for you."

The way she rocked me back and forth made me realize she was for real. Because she wasn't a soft person. Under normal circumstances, Aunt Elba would never hold and rock me while I cried.

Obviously, these weren't normal circumstances. She really planned to send me away.

My world spun like a carnival ride. My stomach lurched, and I put my hand over my mouth, thinking I might throw up.

"You have to be strong, Linda," she said. "You *are* strong. I just want you to grow up with the best."

All of a sudden I was blubbering like a baby. "I want to stay with you," I choked out. "I don't want to live with anyone else. I'll take care of you."

"I know, I know," she soothed, still rocking me back and forth. "It is a hard thing."

But she wasn't saying *Oh, okay, if you feel this way, then forget it.* I could tell from her voice that she wasn't going to change her mind.

I looked up and saw that tears were pooling in the deep bags under her eyes.

Whoa. Aunt Elba never cried.

I sat up, wiped my face on a napkin, and blew my nose. Then I handed a napkin to her. What if she had another stroke from getting upset?

I couldn't fall apart. I had to be strong.

She wiped her eyes, swallowed, and took a deep breath. "I'm still going to see you and be in your life, okay? We'll visit. We're not . . ." Her voice broke.

I handed her another tissue. I didn't trust myself to speak without sobbing.

"We're not losing each other," she went on. "It's just a . . . change. A better future for you."

She was talking about this like it was a done deal. I had to talk her out of it. "What are you going to do for money? Who's going to take care of you? Your car isn't that good. Even if you get a job in Tucson, how will you—"

She straightened her shoulders like a soldier headed off to war. "I'm going to live with *Mamá* and *Papá* for a while."

I froze in the middle of wiping my eyes and stared at her. "But you hate them."

"It's time for me to make my peace."

I studied her suspiciously. "Are you dying? Or . . . are they?"

She put her hand over my mouth. "*Ssh.* No. No, and I will not stay there forever. But a little time in South Texas with them is what I need to decide on my next step."

I started to get mad then. It sounded like Aunt Elba had her whole life plan laid out, only I wasn't included.

But she hadn't thought things through. "You can't just give me away," I said. "You're my guardian, right? And this Pat, this *Cooking from Cans* lady . . . she's hardly even related to me. That can't be legal."

She took a deep breath and laid a hand on my arm. "Actually," she said, "Pat is an adoptive mom and already has a—how to say it?—a home study. From an agency. This would be a something called kinship care, not adoption; but it is perfectly legal."

"You mean you're giving me to her forever?" I scooted back and stared at her. "How long have you known about this?"

"I made things final with Pat and the lawyer today, but I have been thinking about it for a long time," she said. "Oh, my Linda, I wanted to tell you sooner, but I just couldn't."

I wanted to get mad, throw a fit even; but then I looked at her sad face. It was the face of a woman who had loved and cared for me for as long as I could remember. A woman who'd just had a stroke.

So I stuffed my achy, empty, miserable feelings deep inside. "You might as well tell me about this family," I said.

"Well, they're very nice." She took a deep breath and put on a smile. "They're a big family—seven kids. And they have a daughter your age—"

"So they already have enough kids," I interrupted. "Why do they want one more?"

"Pat and her husband have a place in their hearts for others."

"You mean, I'm a good deed to them." I gripped the edge of the table hard. "Why can't I go to Texas with you? I can live with *los abuelos* if you're there. I can handle it."

She shook her head. "I would never do that to a young girl. They are too old, too . . . negative. This family is better for you."

"Where do they live?" I asked, almost as an afterthought. I was expecting her to say Tucson, or maybe Phoenix.

"Pittsburgh," she said.

"*Pittsburgh?* Where the heck is that?"

Chapter Four

Two weeks later I'd not only found Pittsburgh on the map (okay, so maybe I *had* heard of it before), but I was there, approaching a dark and silent house. Beside me was the quiet, preoccupied dad of my new family. He'd picked me up at the airport.

Big trees loomed over three stories of the haunted-looking place. The house was tucked in close together with a bunch of other old houses. I missed the desert horizon I'd seen my whole life.

I missed Aunt Elba.

"Strange," said the dad. "I know they're expecting you." We were standing on the porch.

"SURPRISE!" It sounded like fifty people shouted it as the house's lights came on, blinding me.

The dad patted my shoulder. "Sorry. The usual zoo," he said.

All these people were shouting and laughing and coming toward me, and I took a step backward. That's what I wished I could do for real: step backward into my family of two and my familiar life in Arizona.

But I couldn't. I was here. The WELCOME, LINDA banner now

illuminated on the front porch made it clear that we weren't at the wrong place.

An athletic-looking woman with short, gray hair came toward me, smiling. "Hello, dear. I'm your aunt Pat."

She looked exactly as she had on TV, and she sounded like her voice on the phone . . . but she was still a stranger. To my relief, she didn't hug me but just took my hand and held it while she talked. "Come on in. Sorry about the party. These kids will grab any excuse for one. It's mostly family, anyway."

This was mostly family? I stood still. If most of these kids and teenagers lived in this house, that meant I'd be around them all the time. To me they looked like a crowd of thousands. I couldn't distinguish one from the other.

Then three little boys—one black, one Asian, and one Latino—came running toward us, yelling and batting at one another with plastic swords. The Latino kid veered my way and crashed into me, nearly knocking me over.

"Angel!" Pat scolded, saying it the Anglo way: *Ain-jell.* "That's not how to greet your new sister."

"¡No es mi hermana!" he yelled, and took off after the other kids.

I was with him on that one. I *wasn't* the new sister in this family, and I would have loved to run away. Or maybe hit someone with a plastic sword.

"Can we at least find her a quiet corner?" the dad asked.

"That would be great," I said.

"Of course," Pat said. "And I'll bring you some food. You can meet the family a few at a time."

Pat shepherded me into a corner of the living room and told me how good it was to finally meet me in person. The dad ran interference with the curious kids who kept coming over to look at me. In a couple of minutes Pat came back with a plate of food.

I was famished; but when I looked at what was on the plate, I lost my appetite. Runny macaroni and cheese, bright orange Jell-O salad, green beans in some kind of brown sauce . . . it was like my worst nightmare of a school cafeteria meal. The smell made my already-nervous stomach turn over.

"Thanks." I set down the plate beside me.

Pat and the dad wandered off, and two teenage girls approached me. The blond one, who looked about seventeen or eighteen, gave me a quick hug. "Hi, I'm Jen. Welcome to the family. Do you like the green bean casserole? It's my specialty!"

"It's . . . it looks interesting," I said. "I actually haven't had a chance to—"

"This is Chloe, and she's a freshman, too. She's sharing a room with you. She was the only one of us who didn't have a roommate. Now she won't be lonely anymore."

Chloe rolled her eyes. She had very short, dark hair, a pierced nose, and all-black clothes. She looked as happy about the roommate news as I was.

"Hey," I said to her.

"Hey."

"Well, talk!" Jen grabbed a chair and scooted it close to me, then pushed Chloe down onto it. "Get to know each other. Oh, hi," she called to someone across the room. She turned back to us. "Look, I have to go talk to Mrs. McGinnis. She lives across the street, and I usually babysit for her on Fridays; but this week we have a game. See ya."

Chloe and I scooted our chairs away from each other.

The little boy Angel headed for me again, waving his sword.

I grabbed his arm before he could whack me. "What's up with the swordplay, buddy?" I asked him in Spanish.

"Don't even try to talk to him," Chloe advised as he pulled away and ran off. "He's outta control. Plus, he's just here temporarily, until social services can find him another home. We don't really have room."

Which begged the question: did they have room for me?

She waved her hand toward a group of kids who were engaged in a loud game of knocking over action figures. "If you like little kids, there are plenty of others to fuss over." She made a sour face.

Clearly, Chloe did *not* like little kids. Or even kids her own age. The idea of rooming with her made me feel as dark and depressed as her gloomy outfit.

Still, I decided I'd better make an effort to get along. "So, have you always lived here?"

"Yeah. I'm the only biological offspring."

Weird way to put it, but okay. "Why did your folks adopt so many kids?"

Chloe shrugged. "They can't have any more babies, and they're both from big families. They see it as a 'gift from God' thing." She studied me from head to toe. "Where'd you say you were from?"

"Arizona."

"Guess they dress different out there, huh? And talk different, too."

I looked down at my jeans and loose blouse. "Isn't this how kids dress here?" I didn't say it, but I hoped all the Pittsburgh kids didn't dress like her. Funeral black wasn't my best fashion color.

She snorted. "Hardly. And just a tip: we don't call ourselves kids, either. You're in the city now."

What was that supposed to mean?

"I'm going upstairs. I want a little privacy before my whole life gets invaded." She stood up and walked away.

Great. Obviously she meant I was the invader; but she was gone before I could tell her that I didn't like it any better than she did.

I wanted Aunt Elba so bad that my whole chest ached. I

missed her calloused hands brushing my face or hair; I missed her words of wisdom; I missed the way she was always watching and checking to make sure I was doing what I was supposed to do. I felt so out of place here. And I didn't even have Julia to laugh with about Chloe.

Pat bustled over. "Are you getting enough to eat?" She saw my still-full plate and looked worried. "I hope we're not going to have a problem," she said. "We're an 'eat what's on your plate' kind of family."

"I . . . I guess I'm just not hungry tonight."

"No eating disorder, is there?" She studied me. "You're pretty thin."

"I like to eat, okay?" What I *didn't* like was how she was looming over me. I stood up. "I like to cook, too. Maybe I can help—"

"Sure, I can teach you to cook," Pat said. "It'll be a great way for us to get to know each other."

"Actually, I already—"

Jen approached in time to interrupt. "Yeah, as long as you know who's boss," she joked, putting an arm around Pat. "Mom's kitchen is her kingdom."

"Oh, now, I'm not that bad," Pat said, beaming.

"Mom's famous for her cooking," Jen added brightly. "She taught me how to make the green bean casserole."

"Oh?" I stifled my next question: why would anyone want to teach—or learn—how to make something so revolting?

And Jen *had* to be joking about her mom being famous. Nobody could seriously watch her stupid cooking show, could they?

A white-haired lady joined us with a plate of sugar-dusted pastries in her hand. "Hello, dear. I'm Edith Piotrowski, and I live next door."

And I should care *why*? But Aunt Elba's rules about being

polite to grown-ups, especially old ones, echoed in my ears. "I'm glad to meet you," I lied.

Pat had turned away to resolve a dispute between a couple of school-aged kids, and Mrs. Piotrowski grabbed my elbow. "Here, eat these," she said, shoving the plate of pastries into my hand. "They're paczki. Real Polish doughnuts."

They did look good. I took a bite, and my eyebrows went up. "Wow, is that apricot filling?"

She nodded. "I think this batch isn't so good," she said.

"No, it's delicious."

Pat turned around in time to hear me say that, and a couple of lines appeared on her forehead. "Dessert without dinner?"

"My fault. I forced it on her." Mrs. Piotrowski winked at me. "Such a polite girl."

Pat didn't look convinced. In fact, she opened her mouth like she was about to start lecturing me.

"I think I need to go upstairs," I said before she could start. "It was a long trip."

"Of course, dear," Pat said, her face softening into a sympathetic smile. "Your room's the second door on the right. And the bed's all made."

"Thanks." I backed away, ready to run upstairs.

"You know, Linda," Pat said, reaching out to rub my arm, "we're so glad you're here."

That made me a little teary. Aunt Elba always rubbed my arm or my back in just the same way.

But Pat wasn't done talking. "We feel really blessed that you speak Spanish, too. You'll be a big help with Angel while he's here." She smiled. "God's good, isn't he?"

"Um, yeah," I muttered, and then turned and ran up the stairs.

I found my room; but when I turned the knob, the door was locked. Didn't that just figure? I wasn't ready for a fight with

Chloe, so I sank down on the landing, my head in my hands.

I was starting to get a more complete picture of my new life, and it wasn't exactly cheering me up. It seemed as if Pat had taken me in for my language abilities, not because she really wanted me here. It made sense, but it didn't feel great. And what would happen after Angel moved on to his permanent home?

Was I supposed to move on, too?

Anyway, the people in this family were nice enough—except for my lovely roommate—but they were strangers. I felt as out of place as a jalapeño in a chocolate chip cookie.

The fact that I had to start a brand-new school tomorrow didn't make things any easier. Especially if Chloe was right, and everyone dressed and talked differently from me.

I put my head down on my knees and tried to tell myself that things would be better soon. Too bad I didn't believe my own pep talk.

Linda Delgado

<u>CLICK</u> FOR MORE PICTURES

RELATIONSHIP STATUS:
Single

INTERESTS: Food, friends, more food, fun!

Pittsburgh food so far:
• cafeteria-style mac & cheese (who knew anyone cooked this at home?)
• orange Jell-O with strange canned fruit in it
• green beans in runny brown sauce
• paczki—Polish doughnuts—now these are yummy! I'll post the recipe as soon as I can get it.

Friends/Family/Foodie Comments:
Linda says: So maybe I caught my new family on a bad night, but I'm pretty horrified by my first meal in Pittsburgh.
Julia says: Welcome to the real world, Miss Foodie. You've been spoiled ☺. We eat mac & cheese over here all the time, remember? And you loved it when you were eight!

Chapter Five

"This is where we part ways," Chloe told Jen and me the next morning as we reached the end of our block.

"Aren't you going to school?" I asked. Chloe was unfriendly and weird, but at least she was someone I sort of knew.

"Yeah, but not with you. And don't let on that you're living in my house, okay?"

"Why?" I stood in the swirling leaves and wrapped my arms around myself to keep warm in the October chill. Back in Arizona, it would have been in the high eighties, with a blue sky.

"Chloe's embarrassed of us," Jen said, sighing. "She likes to *pretend* that no one knows how big her family is." I noticed that Jen emphasized the word *pretend*.

"Whatever," Chloe said. "If you see me, don't say hi."

I watched her depart, witchlike in her black trench coat. I'd actually peeked in her closet this morning while she was in the bathroom, just to see if she owned any other colors of clothing. I'd found one white shirt and one pair of gray slacks. I guess that was her party outfit.

We turned the corner, and there it was: my new school. Jen immediately saw people she knew and started waving. "Go to the office first," she told me. "They'll give you your schedule." She headed off toward her friends.

I stared after her for a minute. Back home, Aunt Elba used to drive me to school so that I could sleep a little later and avoid a long bus ride. Neither of us were big talkers in the morning, but we'd listen to the radio and sometimes sing along.

Julia was right. I'd been spoiled. Aunt Elba had treated me like a princess. Now that I was facing a new school alone, I could appreciate what I'd had.

What I'd lost.

And speaking of Julia, what I wouldn't give to have her waiting for me at my locker, ready to share the latest news and a laugh.

But today, no one was waiting for me. Today, I was all alone. I turned and scuffled through the piles of dead leaves to my new school.

I went through the first hours of the morning in a shy blur. My cream-colored gauze blouse was just different enough from the other girls' hoodies to mark me as new. Even more different was the fact that I was entirely alone. Nobody said hello, nobody called out my name, nobody waited for me after class. I did see Jen once, but she was surrounded by girls and didn't even notice me.

I'd lived my whole life out in the sticks of Arizona, attending school with the same group of kids. I was used to fitting in like a native plant. I was used to hearing a mixture of English and Spanish. I was used to walking out into an open courtyard between classes to chat with my friends under a blue sky. Here, I felt closed in by the cement block hallways, the dented gray lockers, and the low-hanging clouds outside the dirty school windows.

Right before lunch, I found my English class in time to grab a seat close to the door. Given that breakfast had been el cheapo cereal and skim milk, I was starving. I hoped to lie low for the next forty minutes and then make a break for the cafeteria . . . not that the smells drifting out from it were all that promising.

"Good news and bad news, class," said the tall, slim, ebony-skinned teacher. Her voice was soft, but everyone stopped talking immediately and found seats.

"I have a research assignment for you to complete in your small groups," she said, "in the library."

Hmmm. If the in-class groups here were anything like those back home, they already had their friendships and alliances and dynamics worked out. For me to enter one of them in October guaranteed I'd be on the outside.

"What's the good news?" a really cute boy called out.

"The good news, Dino, is that you get to analyze a passage of Shakespeare." When he groaned, she cocked her head to one side. "The other good news for your group is, you have a new member. Meet Linda Delgado." She walked over and put her hand on my shoulder. "Dino, please show Linda the way to the library. Group leaders, pick up your assignments on the way out. We'll discuss your results tomorrow."

I walked with the kid named Dino, feeling awkward. Should I talk to him? Would it be better to be quiet?

"Is she a hard teacher?" I asked finally.

He gave me a curious glance. "Where are you from?"

"Arizona. Why?"

"Your accent's different."

My *accent*? I didn't have an accent. Like most kids where I was from, I spoke Spanish at home and English in school, but I'd known English since I was little.

He shrugged. "Pittsburghers have a sort of nasal sound to their voices," he explained. "You don't. Here's the library."

We walked into a large room that looked more up-to-date than the rest of the school. Computer terminals lined one wall, and floor-to-ceiling windows opened out onto the gray Pittsburgh day. The wonderful smell of old books filled the slightly musty air. You couldn't modernize everything.

I saw a familiar dark-and-gloomy sight by the desk. Chloe! She must work in the library. My face broke into a smile; it was such a relief to see someone I knew.

She had been watching us come in; but when she spotted me, she got really busy at her computer. Of course. I wasn't allowed to talk to her.

My group gathered around a table to look at the assignment. "What's this about?" a pretty blonde asked. "I can't understand Shakespeare's language."

The other member, a serious-looking boy wearing a plaid shirt, leaned way too close to her. "What don't you understand, Heather? Maybe I could help."

"Linda and I will check out the shelves and see if there are any books on *Hamlet*," Dino said, grabbing my arm and pulling me toward the stacks. I went along, not minding. There was something I really liked about Dino; and as we walked together, I realized what it was. He *smelled* good!

"Barry has been trying to ask Heather out all year," he explained, nodding back toward the rest of our group. "Maybe today's the day."

I liked that he was willing to support his geeky classmate's efforts. A lot of guys would've teased or made fun of him . . . or tried to get Heather for themselves, given how pretty she was.

"Do you know where the Shakespeare books are?" I asked as we wandered through the stacks.

"No idea," he admitted.

"We could ask the librarian," I suggested.

Dino screwed up one eye. "Bad idea. Mrs. Tripp will talk to us for the entire period without answering our question."

"How about the student assistant?" I said. "Maybe she knows the lay of the land."

Dino looked over at her. "Chloe, the girl in black," he said. "I'm a little afraid."

"Of Chloe?" I looked at him quickly and realized he was smiling. I giggled. It was so tempting to tell him I lived with her.

"If you'll go with me, I might be okay," he said.

"Sure, I'll protect you." All of a sudden I was having fun. Maybe Pittsburgh wouldn't be so bad, I thought.

We headed toward the desk where Chloe was sitting, but Dino stopped to talk to another group of kids who called out to him. I was getting the idea that he was pretty popular, and I could see why. Not only was he super cute (and yummy smelling), but he actually seemed nice.

"What are you doing here?" Chloe whispered as I approached the desk.

"Don't worry, no one knows I know you," I said, rolling my eyes. "We just have a question about where to find some books."

"Well, it'll have to wait," she said. "I'm having a breakthrough with my lyric poem." She turned back to her computer, delicately plucking at her row of earrings.

"Well, what's the deal?" Dino asked as he came up behind me. "Does Chloe hold the key to our problems?"

Chloe smiled and ran her fingers through her dyed-black hair. Apparently the lyric poem could be put on hold for *certain* people. "Let me see what you need," she said in a husky voice.

She studied the assignment, leaning over the library counter. "Okay, you're looking for lit crit. This way."

She pulled a couple of books off the shelves, ran a black fingernail down the first table of contents, and flipped to chapter six. "Here you go," she said. "*Hamlet*. Ophelia's madness scene. This should give you the information you need."

I was impressed with old Chloe. She knew her way around the library. "Thanks," I said; but she ignored me, focusing all of her energy on Dino.

Heather came over, followed closely by Barry; and we clustered around the book. "Let's see, she's talking about all these spices," Dino said.

"Speaking of spices, what have you been cooking?" The words burst out of me before I could censor them. He just smelled so good, and I was starving.

"Cooking?" He frowned and straightened up. "I haven't been cooking."

"No, really. I smell basil, and garlic, and oregano. Not like you've been eating them . . . well, that, too . . . but more like you've been working with fresh herbs."

Chloe, Heather, and Barry all stared at me like I was crazy.

Dino looked annoyed. "I don't know what you're talking about," he said. "I *hate* cooking. I never cook. Wouldn't do it if you paid me a million dollars. Cooking. Me?"

He sounded so upset that everyone turned to stare at him. He was breathing hard, and his face was red. Had I struck a nerve or what?

Chloe seemed to recognize his discomfort. "Jeez, Linda, give us a break. Like you could really smell spices on a person well enough to identify them. . . . What are you, some kind of weirdo?"

I came to my senses then. For a moment I'd forgotten I wasn't at my old school, where everyone knew all about me and my nose.

"Sorry," I said as my face heated.

"The sense of smell is the most primitive part of us," Barry lectured. "It's the primordial basis of attraction. In other words," he said, grinning at Dino, "I think the new girl likes you."

Heather giggled.

Chloe looked furious.

Dino looked hostile.

I wished I could disappear into the stacks and never come out. "It's not th-th-that." An old stammer I thought I'd conquered came back into my voice, and I wondered if my so-called accent was showing, too. "I used to work in a restaurant, that's all. I have a good sense of smell."

"Well, I wouldn't know about any of that," Dino said in a mean way. "It's not like *I* have to work or anything."

Here I'd thought he was nice.

"Let's get this passage figured out so we can get outta here," he said, focusing all his attention on the other two members of our group.

"Linda . . . was that your name? If you're new, you better come up and get registered on the library computer."

I could have thrown my arms around Chloe for giving me a way out of the embarrassing situation. Except that she started to lecture me as soon as we were out of earshot. "What are you thinking, telling Dino Moretti that he smells?"

"I meant it in a good way," I protested. "It's not like I told him he had BO. He really smells good."

"You don't just tell a boy he smells good," she said, shaking her head. "Especially a boy like Dino."

"What's so special about him?" I sulked. We were back at the counter.

"What's special," she said, "is that I've got my plans for him. Get it?" She eyeballed me. "Stay away."

Did she think she was scaring me? I lifted my hands, palms out. "Fine," I said.

But it wasn't.

Chapter Six

One thing you could say about Pat's cooking: she didn't skimp on quantity. That night's casserole of ground beef, kidney beans, tomatoes, and macaroni was in a dish the size of a small washtub.

And if you didn't like the main dish, you were out of luck. Aside from a loaf of white bread, the casserole was it.

I stared at the food. Should I make a scene? Put up a fight against eating it? If I didn't rebel beforehand, would my stomach rebel afterward?

Pat looked around to make sure everyone up and down the long table had been served. Most of the kids I'd met the night before were here, except for a pair of twins, Hector and Veta, who had soccer practice. Everyone else was digging in; and when Pat saw that I wasn't eating, her eyebrows went up. She didn't say anything, but I could tell I was on the food probation list.

Hoping for support, I studied the father of the family, who looked like a mad scientist. His white hair went straight back from a high forehead and fell to his shoulders. Dreamy blue eyes made him seem as if he belonged to another world. I wasn't sure he'd realized that I was the latest member of his family, even though he'd been the one to pick me up at the airport.

One of the boys saw me looking at him. "Don't try to talk to Sir Dad," he advised me as he scooped himself another huge spoonful of the casserole. "He's finishing a book."

"What kind?" I took a cautious bite.

"Sir Dad writes science fiction and fantasy," Jen said, smiling at me. "Wars with aliens and stuff like that."

"Um, hello," Chloe said. "Dad's work is a little more complex than that, not that *you'd* look up from *National Cheerleader Magazine* long enough to notice. He deals with major philosophical and scientific questions."

"Why do you guys call him Sir Dad?" I took another bite and tried to keep from gagging.

Chloe rolled her eyes. "I'm destined to be surrounded by idiots. Can't you tell?"

"Look at him!" Jen whispered, grinning.

I did, and sure enough, he did kind of look like a medieval knight or maybe some ancient wizard. "Oh," I said, and curled my lip at stuck-up Chloe.

One of the younger boys, Isaiah, had been listening to our conversation, and now he turned to his father. "How's the book going, Sir Dad?" he asked. "Did you blow anybody up today?"

The Asian kid, Sam, socked Isaiah in the arm. "Don't ask about his book," he said.

"Quick, somebody change the subject," Jen said, then turned and whispered to me. "He has writer's block a lot. If he doesn't get his next book done on time, his publisher might not give him another contract."

"And then we'll be poor," Sam explained, "and Mom will have to get another job."

"And we won't be able to keep you two!" Isaiah pointed at me with one hand and Angel with the other.

"Isaiah!" Jen's voice was reproachful.

Sweat broke out on my back and a drop of it rolled down between my shoulder blades. Up until now, I'd taken it for granted that I was welcome here and could stay. I'd thought I was the one in control, giving the family a trial run, able to ditch them anytime.

But what if they kicked me out first? What would happen to me? Could I handle living in Texas with my grandparents, who didn't want me around?

I glanced at Angel to see if he understood. His head was down, and he was shoveling food into his mouth like there might not *be* any food tomorrow.

So maybe he did understand.

Pat spoke up. "Dad wrote a chapter today," she said with a sigh, "and the show is going . . . okay. We'll muddle through. Now, can we change the subject, please?"

I was suddenly eager to prove my value. "Did you ever think of putting fresh peppers into this dish?" I asked Pat. Considering how bland it tasted, I thought that was a pretty polite suggestion.

"No," she said.

"Or maybe some sausage." I wiped my mouth, thinking. "You know, the spicy kind?"

"Well, that's a thought," Pat said, "but everything I cook is pretty much from cans."

"Um, yeah." I tried for tact and a perky, helpful, Jen-like attitude. "If it's too much work to shop for fresh stuff, I could help," I offered.

"No, thanks." Pat flashed a smile at me. "I've got my system, and it seems to work best if I do the cooking myself."

Jen started laughing. "I can't believe you're giving Mom cooking advice. That's so funny!"

"Why? I mean, I know I'm young, but I did work in a restaurant—"

"But Mom is a TV chef and wrote a book about cooking. She's, like, this celebrity."

"Yeah, we're all on TV sometimes," volunteered one of the boys.

I looked down at the unappetizing blob on my plate and then up at the rest of the family. They had to be messing with my head. Except each and every one of them looked perfectly serious.

"So . . . that's a popular show around here?" I asked, trying not to sound completely skeptical.

"Used to be top-rated three weeks out of four on Channel Eight," Pat said.

"And it will be again," Jen added with a loyal smile to Pat.

"Oh." I didn't know what to say.

Sir Dad seemed to shake himself awake. "That's what lets us live in this luxury," he said, waving his arms around to indicate the small, crowded dining room.

I pushed a forkful of casserole from one side of my plate to another and tried to look at the bright side. If I got kicked out and was sent to Texas, maybe I could get a decent meal. And if I stayed, at least I wouldn't gain weight!

Then I wondered: what would the folks on FabFoodz think about *this* recipe? The very thought made me giggle into my napkin. To cover my semihysteria, I grabbed a slice of bread and tried to spread butter on it. The butter was cold and hard, straight out of the refrigerator; and the bread was the flimsy stuff, so it tore instantly. How hard would it be for Pat to get the butter out a half hour before dinner to bring it to room temperature?

Texas was looking better and better.

Jen focused her one-hundred-megawatt smile on me. "So how was your first day at school?"

"Aside from math, classes are fine." I figured I'd better hedge my bets and show Pat that I could fit in and hold a conversation.

"But it'll probably take a while to make friends."

"Maybe you could get involved with First Formal," Jen suggested. "It's right after Thanksgiving, and it's the highlight of ninth grade."

"I don't know anything about the dance," I said, "but I doubt I'll get asked, being new."

"Don't be too sure," Jen said. "Sometimes the boys in school will go for a new girl. You're really cute."

"But she dresses like a dork," Chloe said, "and you should see how she acts around boys."

My face got hot. "At least I don't look and act like every day is a funeral."

We glared at each other.

"Chloe, you and Linda are on dishes tonight," Pat said. "Could you show her where everything is?"

"It's bad enough I have to share my room with her," Chloe grumbled. "Do I have to spend every single minute all day with her, too?"

"Chloe!"

I got up and started picking up dishes, glad to escape the bad food and tension.

"Not so many at once!" Pat cried as I stacked more plates onto my arm.

Why did she have to criticize me even when I was helping her out? "I've been carrying big loads of dishes since I was, like, seven years old," I said. I spun around toward the kitchen.

And ran right into Chloe, who was carrying the giant casserole dish.

"Hey, look out!" she yelled.

The casserole dish went flying. Macaroni and kidney beans and tomatoes and ground beef streaked across the floor and up the white baseboards.

I tried to keep a grip on my stack of plates, reeling and

juggling. I could have done it except that my foot slipped on the casserole mess. I teetered for a breathless moment and then crashed down to the floor. I managed to protect most of the plates with my body, but at least one dropped and shattered beside me.

"Oh, man," and "Look out," and "What a mess" came from the crowd at the table.

"Torpe, torpe," sang Angel.

He called me clumsy! I shook tomato sauce off my hands, glared into his dark eyes, and told him—in Spanish—what he could do with his little remark.

In response he took a big handful of the casserole and rubbed it in his own hair.

"Now look what you did." Chloe stood over me. "Could you watch where you're going?"

"How was I supposed to know you were right behind me?" I hollered back.

"Try opening your eyes."

"Try holding on to your dish. If you hadn't dropped it—"

"Girls!" Pat yelled, loud enough that we both shut up and looked at her. Then she put her head down in her arms.

"Jeez, what a couple of klutzes," one of the boys said.

"Macaroni-hair," Angel said, laughing and sprinkling more macaroni onto his own dark head.

"Cállate," I growled.

Chloe added a swear word I wouldn't have dared say at the table.

"That will do, Chloe," said the father. I'd practically forgotten about him, but apparently our giant catastrophe was enough to make him wake up and notice. "Isaiah, Sam, and Angel: since you're so energized by the situation, you may take over cleanup. Chloe and . . ." He hesitated.

"Linda," Pat supplied without lifting her head.

"Chloe and Linda, go to your rooms."

"We *share* a room, Dad," Chloe whined, "and I'm *not* going up there with her. I can't stand her!"

"Do what I said, young lady." There was no trace of friendliness in his voice.

Chloe's face twisted like a toddler who'd been scolded, and her eyes went shiny. Instantly I realized that she was crazy about her father and hated to look bad in his eyes.

"This is your fault," she hissed at me as her tears overflowed. All that heavy black mascara made spider trails down her face. "You'll be sorry you ever moved here."

But I'd beat her on that one. I already was.

Chapter Seven

"Hey, that's mine!" Chloe bounced off her bed to grab the lamp I'd disconnected.

"Great. Take it." Made to look sooty and antique, it gave out almost no light. A typically depressing accessory in this totally depressing room.

We'd only been shut up in there for five minutes, but between Chloe's glares and the decor, I was about ready to jump out the window. It was bad enough that I'd been moved away from everything I'd known and loved. I missed Aunt Elba's tough love, and, even more, the way she really *knew* me. I missed my friends. I missed the bright sunshine of my Arizona home.

I missed being able to make myself feel better by messing around in the kitchen, putting together some yummy concoction that would amaze Aunt Elba and satisfy my taste buds.

I'd always felt a little weird not having much of a family, especially in my part of the country, where most kids had brothers and sisters and grandparents and aunts and uncles they were close to. Sometimes I'd even wished for a big family. Now I was stuck in the middle of one, and I hated it. Maybe I was suited to being a loner, with only an old, eccentric aunt as a family. Maybe that was why God had taken away my mom when I was a baby. Maybe I didn't deserve a family.

Maybe I'd never fit in anywhere.

I got out my phone and looked at it for a couple of minutes. Aunt Elba had said I should only call when I really needed to talk, because we'd gotten a limited-minutes plan to save money. But tonight I really did need to talk.

When she answered, though, I could hear horns honking and Old Abuela's scolding voice in the background. "Where are you, Aunt Elba?" I asked.

"We're driving to the doctor in Houston. Let me pull over."

Aunt Elba would never talk on the phone while she drove. I listened to more traffic noises and wondered why she'd be driving to the doctor at dinnertime. Then I remembered the time difference. It was late afternoon, not evening, in Texas.

"Are you okay, my Linda?" she asked.

"Yeah, I'm okay." I looked at Chloe hunched over her notebook, writing furiously. How could I talk with her in the room? But we'd been sent here by Sir Dad, and I was afraid to leave. I went into the closet and shut the door. "But Aunt Elba, these people are kind of strange."

"Are they mistreating you?" She sounded mad, like she was going to come over here and beat them up.

"No, not really. But I'm not . . ." I trailed off. In the background, I could hear Old Abuela's irritable voice again, now joined by a deeper one that must be my grandfather's.

Poor Aunt Elba. She hated driving in traffic, and there she was driving her difficult parents to the doctor. "How are things going with you?" I asked.

"Oh, I'm having a few symptoms again," she said, sounding impatient, "so my new doctor here wants me to come in for more tests."

No way. She was seeing the doctor for herself. I'd assumed she was taking her ancient parents to the doctor. Was she sicker than she was letting on?

"Praises to Our Lady that you're settled in there," she continued. "These doctors, they talk about time-consuming treatments for me. Lifestyle changes. Exercise programs!"

I had to laugh at that. Aunt Elba hated the very idea of exercising. But on the other hand, she was always moving: cleaning, cooking, fussing over me. Or at least that's what she used to do.

"I couldn't do the job of caring for you now. If it wasn't for your *tía* Pat, I'm afraid . . ." She trailed off, and I heard traffic and cranky voices in the background.

"What, Aunt Elba?" I had to know. "What would happen to me if it weren't for Pat?" *Or if it didn't work out with Pat.*

"Oh, my Linda, I hear such horrors of the foster care system. I wouldn't like for you to be in it, even for a little while."

"But I thought if I . . . if things didn't work out here . . . I could come home to you. Couldn't I?"

"No, no! I am too sick. It wouldn't be fair to you. Listen to me, Linda. You must be a good child there. You must keep our Pat happy. You can't return to me right now, not with every-thing these doctors are telling me. In fact," she continued, "we're running a little late because of all this traffic. So if it's not an emergency . . ."

"No emergency," I said, trying to keep my voice steady. "I just wanted to hear your voice."

"Oh, my *cara*. We will talk more soon, okay?"

"Sure," I said. "Maybe tomorrow."

I clicked off the phone and sat there, stunned, my arms

wrapped around my middle. Until now I hadn't really believed I was stuck here. I'd thought that if things got too bad, I could run back to Aunt Elba with my tail between my legs, that enough begging and whining and crying would get me out of Pittsburgh.

But Aunt Elba made it sound as though, if things didn't work out with Pat, I'd go into foster care! Which just didn't bear thinking about. I drew in a deep breath, clenched my jaw, and walked out of the closet.

Not that our room was much different from the closet, at least in the level of light and cheerfulness. Jeez, gloomy Chloe and her gloomy room were going to totally bring me down unless I did something fast.

I'd learned from Aunt Elba that when you felt down, action would always make you feel better.

I pulled a box out from under my bed. It was full of nonessential stuff that suddenly felt totally essential. I opened it and took out five stuffed animals: Bappy, the frog I'd had since I was a baby; a cute raccoon my first crush had won for me at the county fair; two Mexican cloth dolls Aunt Elba had bought for me when I'd gotten all As in first grade; and my teddy bear, Arthur. I piled them on top of my white bedspread.

Immediately the room felt more homey. But it wasn't enough.

"So we haven't outgrown the stuffed animals, huh?" Chloe asked in a snide voice.

Ignoring her, I walked over to the window on my side of the room. I studied the hardware for a minute and then unhooked the curtain rods and took down the heavy purple curtains.

"Hey," she said. "What do you think you're doing? People can see in."

"Hang on." I dug through my suitcase until I found an old skirt in reds, blues, and golds. I used my nail scissors to open the waistband, pulled out the elastic, and slid the rod through the belt tunnel. "Voilà," I said. "New curtains."

"All kinds of light is gonna come through that," she complained.

"My point exactly. I can't live in a cave."

"I have very sensitive eyes."

"Well, I'm about to come down with a major case of seasonal affective disorder," I said. I'd just learned about SAD in health class, and the clinical symptoms seemed pretty close to how I felt right now: depressed, sleepy, hopeless.

Chloe grumped and groused to her notebook, where she was undoubtedly writing reams of depressing poetry.

I waited until I was sure she wasn't looking and scooped her stash of foul-smelling incense into the trash. Then I dug through my box until I found a rose-scented Guadalupe candle and put it out on my dresser. I lit it with one of Chloe's matches, and the sweet scent reminded me of home, where Aunt Elba had always burned Guadalupes.

Then I pulled out my collection of cookbooks. Even though Aunt Elba and I knew our usual recipes by heart, I liked reading the books for ideas. Every year since I was about eight, I'd asked for and gotten a cookbook for Christmas. I ran my hands over the food-stained *Latino Kids Cook!* We'd had a lot of fun with that one.

Now the closest I was likely to get to cooking was reading about it.

I swallowed the lump in my throat, shelved the cookbooks, and dug through the box again. I shook out the colorful shawl Julia had given me when she'd come back from the reservation last summer. I ran my fingers over its rough wool, trying to bring back the sensation of her friendship. It would liven up my white bedspread, I decided, and spread it out.

Thinking about Julia reminded me of FabFoodz.com, and I

walked over to the computer beside Chloe's bed. "Can I use this sometime?"

"No way," she said. "There's a homework computer in the dining room. That's what you can use."

"But the boys are always on it."

She shrugged. "Dad got this for me for Christmas," she said, "because I needed it for my writing."

Why didn't that surprise me? Man, I thought only children were supposed to be all selfish with their stuff; but from what I'd seen, kids who had lots of brothers and sisters were even more that way.

Oh, well. Maybe I could find out her password and get online when she was out, if she ever did go out.

I was unwrapping my collection of framed photos—of Aunt Elba; of me and my friends last Halloween; of our old cook, Juan, and his family—when Chloe flung her journal to the floor. It made a loud bang.

"What are you doing?" she asked. "What are you doing to this place?"

I didn't look at her. "Just getting out my stuff. Making the room a little more like home."

"It's *my* room." Her voice sounded sulky and defeated, like she knew she couldn't get away with the argument.

"It *was* yours. For better or worse, now it's ours."

She flopped back onto her bed and stared at the ceiling. "I wish you hadn't come."

"Me, too."

She stared at me. "You mean you don't want to be here?"

"Of course not," I said. "I had a better life out west."

"But I heard you were poor. And had to work all the time."

"Yeah, but it was my life, you know? And people cared about me. I had my friends. And my aunt."

"Who gave you away. And why were you living with her, anyway, not your parents?"

"Shut up." The black cloud inside me, the one that was usually pretty small, started billowing up. "I don't want to talk about it."

"I bet," she said.

I couldn't tell if she was being nasty or was pitying me. Either way, it felt bad. I lined up my photos, but my mood was sinking fast.

There was a knock on the door.

"Don't come in," Chloe said halfheartedly.

The door opened a few inches. "Everybody decent?" asked her dad.

An expression of joy and hope flashed across Chloe's face. She leaned down and picked up her notebook. "We're decent," she said. "I was just doing some writing."

"Want to show it to me?" he asked, and it was clear that he was trying to make up with her.

"Oh, all right," she said. Her show of reluctance was belied by the speedy way she gathered her stuff and strutted out of the room with him.

I sank down on my bed and looked around. My changes had made the room a little less cavelike and a little prettier, but it wasn't anything like my sunny room in Arizona.

And *I* didn't have a dad to come cheer me up.

Clearly, my life here wasn't going to be quite like my life in Arizona. But maybe there were some other changes I could make, changes that would make me feel more like myself.

Of course, the number one way to do that, for me, was cooking. I just had to find a way to express myself through food—and the sooner, the better.

I went downstairs, gave Sam five dollars to tell me Chloe's password, and got on her computer.

FABFOODZ.COM

HOME | PROFILE | FRIENDS | RECIPES

Linda Delgado

<u>CLICK</u> FOR MORE PICTURES

RELATIONSHIP STATUS:
Single

INTERESTS: Food, friends, more food, fun!

Recipe for a disastrous dinner:

- Generic macaroni
- Giant can kidney beans
- Giant can tomatoes
- Ground beef (preferably not organic)

Mix and serve with white bread and cold butter. Watch your kids gag and get into fights. This stuff looks especially attractive spilled all over your dining-room floor.

Friends/Family/Foodie Comments:

Julia says: Sounds like a story. Poor baby! Hang in there!

Chapter Eight

"¡Quiero café! ¡Quiero café!"

"Angel. Be quiet!"

The next day, a Saturday, I pulled my pillow over my head and tried to continue sleeping through the bilingual argument coming from downstairs.

"¡Te odio!" There was a crash, and a yell.

It was so much like our worst nights at the restaurant that I rolled out of bed and stumbled down the stairs to see what was going on.

When I reached the kitchen, Pat was wiping coffee off her face and neck, her jaw clenching with the effort to maintain control.

Angel crouched in front of the cupboards, his face streaked with tears, chanting "I hate you" and calling Pat very nasty names in Spanish.

"Um . . . good morning?"

At the sound of my voice, both of them turned to me with similar snarls that made me want to run back to bed. But when she recognized me, Pat's face relaxed a little and she beckoned me in. "Maybe you can tell me what he's saying. He's very upset. He wants to drink coffee, which is the last thing he needs."

"You threw coffee at her?" I asked Angel in Spanish.

"*Sí, sí. Quiero café. Mi mamá . . .*" He trailed off and started cursing at Pat again, swiping tears from his cheeks.

"I was just down here trying to get a minute's peace before the whole house woke up, drinking my coffee, and he exploded into here and tried to grab the cup out of my hands. Then he started talking a mile a minute, all in Spanish. Pointing at the coffeepot. I don't know what brought this on."

I looked at Angel. Something about the still way he sat made me suspect that he understood every word Pat was saying.

"Um . . . maybe he could have a little *café con leche*? With a lot of sugar? That's how Aunt Elba used to make it for me."

"But the caffeine . . . and he's already so active . . ."

"There's not much caffeine the way you make it for kids," I explained. "Here. I'll show you."

"But I hate to reward him for . . ." She sighed, looked down at him, and lifted her hands. "Sure. I didn't realize it was common to give young children coffee in your culture."

I poured some milk into a cup, frowning. Did Angel and I have the same culture? I mean, we both spoke Spanish; but I was pretty sure I'd been raised totally different from him otherwise.

For instance, I'd never say anything as disrespectful to a grown-up as what he was muttering under his breath even now. "*Basta!*" I said to him, sharply. "Treat her with respect. She is taking care of you."

He kicked my ankle hard enough that I yelled. In a flash I was on the floor, squeezing his scrawny little shoulders, chewing him out.

I felt Pat's hand on my arm, and I stood up, breathing hard. "I'm sorry, Pat. It's just that . . . that really hurt!"

"Oh, I know," she said. "He can be a holy terror."

I stuck the half-full cup of milk in the microwave and grimaced at her. "Why do you put up with it?"

She chuckled. "Every kid who comes to stay with us acts out in some way or another. You get used to it. Although I have to admit, when he threw hot coffee at me, I was about to lose it. He's got quite an arm."

"Quite a kick, too." Our eyes met, and I raised my eyebrows. "Future sports star?" We both giggled. For just a minute we were on the same wavelength: two people suffering through a kid's bratty behavior.

I pulled the hot milk out of the microwave, poured a little coffee into the cup, and added a couple of spoonfuls of sugar. "Voilà. *Café con leche* for kids."

She studied it dubiously. "I still think caffeine and sugar are about the worst combination for a kid like Angel."

"He says his mother gave it to him. Maybe it'll help him, you know, feel at home."

Pat brightened. "And that trumps the good-health guidelines every time." She gave me a little smile and held out her hands to Angel. "Thanks for helping out, Linda."

"Sure." I patted Angel's back as Pat pulled him into a hug. Once again our eyes met, and I felt that tiny click of understanding between us.

"It's not every day that I allow the kids to cook in *my* kitchen," she said as I turned to go back upstairs. Emphasis on the *my*.

Now why did she have to go and ruin everything? And I wouldn't even have considered making *café con leche* cooking.

It was only as I walked up the stairs that I realized another implication of what she'd said.

If every kid who moved in here acted out in some way . . . did that include me?

I tried to go back to sleep, but by now some of the other kids were waking up and I was pretty wide-awake myself. So I took my phone out onto the front porch—the only place to escape the noise of this family. I could hear the distant sounds of Angel, Sam, and Isaiah fighting over what channel to watch, but I could also hear birds singing.

One thing about Pittsburgh: there were a lot of trees; and now, in the middle of October, they were gorgeous shades of gold and red. I'd seen pictures of this kind of autumn before, but in person it was a lot more vivid. The crisp air made me glad I'd worn a sweater, and I scooted into a patch of sun to warm my legs. A lot of the neighbors, including old Mrs. Piotrowski, who'd fed me Polish pastries my first night here, had put out pumpkins or scarecrows or colorful fall flags. There was nothing on our porch.

If Pat ever got the time and energy to decorate, how would she do it? Set out a couple of giant cans of mashed pumpkin?

On a Saturday at home, I'd have been cooking in the restaurant with Aunt Elba. I wondered about our customers. Had they found another place to eat on their Friday night trips to Mexico? Did they miss the friends and good food from our restaurant, or were they just as glad to grab a take-out burrito at Tacos & Toppings?

It was hard to believe that whole life of mine was gone. My heart hurt inside my chest again, and before I could start crying, I punched in Aunt Elba's number.

"How are you, *cara mia*?" she asked, and I poured out all my complaints: about the food, about gloomy Chloe and loudmouthed Angel, about how hard math was at school.

When I finally stopped talking, she didn't say anything.

"Aunt Elba?" I asked.

When she still didn't answer, I got scared. Had I over-whelmed her with all of my problems? Did she have another stroke? "Aunt Elba, say something."

She cleared her throat. "Linda. I didn't raise you to complain about every little thing. When you are feeling sad, what should you do?"

"Um ... call you?" I tried for a joke.

She didn't laugh. "You're old enough to depend on yourself. Now, I want you to find something to do. Make yourself useful. Make things better. Cook something!"

"But Pat doesn't want me to cook," I whined. "And even if she did, there's no decent food here."

"You're a big girl, Linda. Now shape up. Remember how I raised you, and find a way to feel better."

"But Aunt Elba—"

"I will talk to you in three days. Not before. And I expect to hear from you good things that you've done with your time. Understand?"

"I understand," I growled, and flipped shut the phone. A lot of help she was.

On the bright side, Aunt Elba must be feeling at least a little better if she was going back to tough-love mode.

I stood and looked up and down the street, pushing my hands into my back and then stretching. I hadn't even had breakfast, because there wasn't anything decent to eat. But just then I caught a good smell coming out of Mrs. Piotrowski's house next door. An idea formed in my mind.

I went inside to get scissors and an old can—there were plenty of those around!—and peeled off the paper label. Then I walked around Pat's weedy yard, cutting cool-looking branches with red berries, tall golden stalks of grasses, and some dried purple flowers. I stuck my findings into the can, then ran upstairs and raided Jen's hair accessories to find a pretty brown-and-gold ribbon to tie around the can.

"What're you doing?" Angel asked, sidling close.

"None of your business." I nudged—okay, shoved—him away. Luckily, Jen and Chloe were still asleep and Pat was off somewhere, so they couldn't nose into my activities.

I took my creation over to Mrs. Piotrowski's house and knocked on her front screen door. The good smells were even stronger up close.

Mrs. Piotrowski came to the door wearing a big stained apron, her gray hair pushed back in a headband and her cheeks pink.

"Hi. I brought you something." I held out the dried-flower arrangement.

"Well, aren't you sweet. Come on in." She held open the door, and I walked inside. "You're Linda, aren't you?"

I nodded. "Whatever you're cooking sure smells good." I was shameless!

"Come back to the kitchen, and you can test my pumpkin bread," she said.

Score! I was already feeling so much better. Aunt Elba was right. I had to take action to solve my own problems.

Mrs. Piotrowski led me through an old-lady living room, then a dining room with a big round wooden table that had a bowl of fresh fruit and the *Pittsburgh Post-Gazette* on it. She set my vase there. "Now doesn't that look nice," she said. "My kids and their kids come over every Sunday, and I'm cooking ahead because I have a date tonight."

"Lucky you," I said, smiling. "Is it a first date?"

"Yes, and I *am* lucky," she said. "A nice man from my parish with season tickets for the Penguins. We'll go to mass and then the hockey game."

"Wow." I'd sort of expected that she wouldn't have much of a life, but her weekend plans outshone mine by a mile.

"Let me get you some pumpkin bread, and then you can watch me roll out my pierogi dough." Her kitchen was small, but obviously a cook's kitchen. She had pans hanging overhead and pumpkin bread cooling on a rack. A big pot was boiling on the stove, and onions bubbled in butter.

My stomach growled. I wanted that bread, and truthfully, whatever else she was cooking, too.

She started to cut me some warm pumpkin bread and then paused in the act of putting it on a plate. "Your aunt Pat knows you're over here, doesn't she?"

"Um, not exactly." I stared at the bread, inhaling its aroma, salivating for the real butter that perched on a saucer beside it. "But I'm sure she wouldn't mind."

"Oh, dear." She frowned. "Pat's so particular about knowing where her children are. Maybe you'd better run over there and let her know you'll be here."

"Oh, it'll be fine." I reached out for the bread plate, trying to assume a casual air. If I didn't get a bite soon, I'd pass out from starvation.

"Well . . . are you sure she won't be upset?"

"I'm sure. And if I don't get a bite of this pumpkin bread right now, I'll lose my mind!"

She threw back her head and laughed. "All right, then, eat away." She handed me the butter dish and a knife. I carried it to her dining-room table, salivating from the delicious smell.

There was a pounding on the door. "*Hola*, Mrs. P!" yelled a too-familiar voice.

Angel.

"Would you get that, dear?" Mrs. Piotrowski asked.

I put down my pumpkin bread, went to the door, and glared at Angel through the screen. "What do you want?"

"We're not supposed to bother the neighbors," Angel told me in Spanish.

"I'm not bothering her, but you are," I said, eager to get back to my food. "Go home."

"If I go home, I'm telling on you."

I thought uneasily of what Mrs. Piotrowski had said about Pat needing to know where we were at all times. "Then what do you want?"

"I want to come in," he said, his big, beautiful brown eyes staring up at me. "There's nothing to do at home, and the boys won't play with me. Isaiah hit me with a bat." He held out his arm; and sure enough, there was an ugly red knot on it.

I sighed. "Fine, you can come in for a minute. Maybe Mrs. Piotrowski will give you some pumpkin bread. But then you have to go home, okay?" I didn't want Angel ruining my plan, which wasn't just to get a delicious breakfast, but to find out if I could do some cooking over here.

"Okay," he said with a sweet smile that I didn't trust for a minute.

I led him back to the kitchen. "Do you know Angel?" I asked Mrs. Piotrowski.

"Of course I do." She gave him a sidearm hug. "How are you, dear? Would you like some pumpkin bread?" She gestured toward it.

He wrinkled his nose. "*¿Se me gusta?*" he asked me.

"You'll love it." I cut him a piece and grabbed a plate from the cupboard where Mrs. Piotrowski had gotten my plate.

Angel stuffed the bread into his mouth without even sitting down at the table. I took my time with my slice, closing my eyes to savor the flavors and try to figure out the spices. "Is there allspice in here?" I called to Mrs. Piotrowski, who was banging pans in the kitchen.

"Yes, there is." She came out carrying a big ball of dough wrapped in plastic wrap. "You like it?"

"*¡Sí!*" Angel hollered. He never seemed to say anything in

a normal voice. "Can I have more?" He asked this in English, confirming my suspicion that he knew more than he'd admitted at Pat's house. While he spoke, he was pushing himself up, arms stiff, onto her table, which started to tip.

I grabbed the plates, and Mrs. Piotrowski grabbed the fruit bowl. "Angel!" I scolded.

"We need to put that energy to work," Mrs. Piotrowski said. "Angel, I'm going to show you how to mash potatoes."

Was she nuts? No way would I let the kid do anything of the sort.

On the other hand, if she'd let Angel help . . . I went to the kitchen doorway and watched as she found a footstool for Angel to stand on and set him to work pushing an old-fashioned potato masher up and down. "I can roll out the dough, if you'll show me how," I offered.

"That would be wonderful. You children are such a blessing."

So I rolled the dough out thin and used a drinking glass to cut circles. Mrs. Piotrowski grated cheese and showed Angel how to mix it up with the onions and mashed potatoes to make a filling. Then we all sat and put teaspoonfuls of filling on the dough circles, folded over the dough, and sealed the half circles closed by pushing a fork around the edges.

In the middle of it, Angel got bored and ran home, but I stayed until we had dozens of little pierogi pillows done.

"Now I'm going to wrap these and boil them tomorrow," she said. "I can't thank you enough for your help. Come over tomorrow afternoon if you get the chance, and you can taste what you helped make."

"I will," I said, already plotting how I'd escape without Pat noticing. I only wished I didn't have to sneak to fulfill my passion. I hadn't quite worked up the nerve to ask Mrs. Piotrowski about cooking some of my recipes here, but maybe tomorrow. I'd find a way to keep cooking, one way or another.

When I got back to Pat's house, I tried to slip up to my room, but she cornered me. "Where have you been?"

"I, um . . ." I felt my face turn red. "Next door," I mumbled. Why was she making me feel guilty, like I'd been kissing boys and smoking pot? "I was just helping Mrs. Piotrowski with some stuff."

"Well. I want you to check with me next time before you go."

I glared at her. No way was I checking each time. Especially when there were hot pierogi to taste!

But then Aunt Elba's voice came to me: *You must be a good child there. You must keep our Pat happy.* "Okay, sure, sorry," I grouched, and ran up the stairs.

I never did get a chance to duck out the next day for Mrs. Piotrowski's pierogi.

Linda Delgado

CLICK FOR MORE PICTURES

RELATIONSHIP STATUS:
Single

INTERESTS: Food, friends, more food, fun!

What I'm cooking today: Pierogi!

What else I'm doing: Collecting dead grass and leaves to make decorations for my new, gloomy room

Friends/Family/Foodie Comments:

Julia says: WTH are pierogi?

Linda says: Polish pasta stuffed with mashed potatoes, cheese, and onions.

Julia says: I thought your new family only cooked from cans.

Linda says: I found a foodie next door—woo-hoo!

Julia says: Yay!

Julia Payette

CLICK FOR MORE PICTURES

RELATIONSHIP STATUS: Single

INTERESTS: Reading, computers, cooking. (Yeah, I'm a geek.)

What I'm cooking today: Hot dogs for my bratty little brothers

What else I'm doing: Crying because my BFF moved away!

Friends/Family/Foodie Comments:

Linda says: I'm crying too—I miss you!

Julia says: I made Mom drive by your restaurant and it's all boarded up with a for-sale sign. Boo-hoo!

Linda says: Maybe we could buy it and start our own restaurant.

Misty says: I wish you would! My dad and me used to come eat your burritos—they rock!

Linda says: Hey Misty, I remember you.

Julia says: Me too—we were in homeroom together. Want to skip assembly and go get brunch sometime?

Linda says: No fair! I want to come too!

Julia says: Aw, I know, Linda! Miss you so much!

Chapter Nine

Finally, on Monday I got to the class I'd been waiting for: Food Science. I was excited to be in a school that actually *had* Food Science, and thrilled about another chance to cook until . . . I saw Chloe approaching the same classroom at the same time.

So far we'd been lucky enough not to have any classes together. It so sucked that this class, my likely favorite, would be ruined by the Queen of Gloom herself.

"Remember, you don't know me," she hissed as we walked through the doorway.

Works for me, I thought.

When I saw Dino from my English class, my heart beat a little faster. Guys in a cooking class? Yeah, apparently.

My own hot-and-bothered reaction annoyed me. Dino was cute; but ever since I'd made the mistake of telling him he smelled good, he'd totally ignored me. I'd also noticed that he got extra mouthy when he knew other kids were listening and spent a lot of time combing his hair. So I was trying my best not to like him. Most of the time I succeeded.

The teacher, Miss Xavier, looked over my paperwork and then assigned me to Kitchen Six.

Kitchen Six consisted of two tall, blond clones . . . and Dino.

So that was my next challenge: to not like Dino while cooking with him. Oh, well. At least I wasn't stuck in Chloe's kitchen.

"All right, class," the teacher said, clapping her hands to get our attention. "We've been learning about proper eating habits as well as broiling, boiling, sautéing, and baking. I'd like each kitchen to plan a dish to cook that incorporates principles of healthy eating as well as one of the cooking techniques we've learned."

The blondes, Dino, and I sat down around the little table in Kitchen Six. Dino acted like I was invisible. No big surprise, but still it kind of hurt my feelings.

The girls were friendly enough, introducing themselves as "Mindy and Mandy—no relation!" They wanted to bake a no-calorie cake that had appeared in *Fabulous and Fifteen* magazine. "It's made with cake mix and diet soda," Mindy, or Mandy, explained.

"One of my friends at the gym made it, and she said it's really good," said the other one. Apparently both Mindy and Mandy helped out at Mindy's mom's gym in their spare time.

"What do you guys think?" they asked, turning to us.

Dino wasn't listening. He'd been folding a complicated paper airplane and was in the process of launching it at his buddies across the room.

Rats. I'd hoped he would disagree with the diet cake idea. It was hard for a new girl to make waves, but a cake made with diet soda sounded like a tragedy to me.

"Dino!" One of the blondes grabbed his arm. "Pay attention. You're going to get our kitchen another demerit."

I raised my eyebrows. "Group grading?"

"Yes, and Dino's our downfall," complained the one I was starting to identify as Mandy.

"Now," said the other one—Mindy?—in a flirty, scolding voice, "what do you think of our cake idea?"

Dino shrugged. "Doesn't matter to me," he said.

"Of course, you probably have a cook at home," Mandy cooed to him. "And you're soooo muscular. You don't need to worry about your weight. But for us girls . . ."

Dino turned red, like their comments embarrassed him.

His friend chose that moment to toss back the paper airplane, which hit Dino in the side of the head. He jumped up and fired it back in a show-offy way that the teacher couldn't help but see.

"Mr. Moretti," she said, approaching our table. "Is there a shortage of work here, that you feel the need to find other activities?"

He shrugged.

"You know, class participation is part of your grade; and that means participating in the planning work of the group. I hope the four of you have made some progress."

"Oh, we have," I assured her. "We've almost decided." I shot Dino a dirty look to show him that I didn't think his paper airplane was at all cute or anything.

"So, what do you guys think?" Mandy asked. "Are we on for the cake?"

I breathed in for courage. "Um, shouldn't we make something that, well, tastes good? Like bread, or something? It could be whole grain if you're worried about your diet. . . ."

Mindy made an X with her forefingers. "No carbs!"

"But cake mix has carbs. . . ." I looked at Dino, hoping for some support, but naturally he just shrugged.

"Let's vote," Mandy suggested. "Who wants to make the diet cake?"

She and Mindy both raised their hands, of course. Dino

shrugged again, then lifted his hand. "That's cool," he said.

Then Mindy and Mandy sat there discussing abs and pecs and biceps—their own, and those of people they knew—until Miss Xavier called out, "Listen up, folks."

"I hope you all have your meals planned out," she said. "We'll do ingredient lists next time. I have one more exciting announcement before class ends." She paused dramatically. "Class, we've been chosen to provide refreshments for First Formal!"

The class greeted this news with silence.

"It's a great opportunity to showcase your skills," she continued in a determined, cheerful voice.

"Yeah, only some of us are *going* to the dance," Mindy said. "The last thing we want is to be stuck behind the refreshment table."

"If anyone is having trouble in the class," Miss Xavier said, "this is an opportunity to earn extra credit. And may I remind you that this is a required class. Failure means you have to repeat it next year."

"Yo, Dino," one of the guys in another kitchen called.

Dino gave a rueful grin.

I cocked my head at him, surprised. Okay, he acted a little crazy in this class—completely different from how he acted in English—but he seemed bright. Too bright to fail an easy class like cooking.

"Dino!" someone else called.

The teacher looked our way. "Should I sign you up, Mr. Moretti?" she asked.

He grinned. "Sure."

"But he'll want to go to the dance," Mandy pouted.

Dino lifted his hands, palms up. "I gotta pass this class," he said.

"He'll probably poison all of us," another guy said.

"Other volunteers?" asked the teacher. She looked sort of disappointed in us.

A flashbulb went off in my head. I'd been looking for a chance to cook, and here was one falling into my lap. I raised my hand. "I can do it." To Mindy and Mandy I said, "Nobody's going to ask a new girl to a dance, anyway. I may as well."

"Told you she liked you, Moretti," one of Dino's friends teased.

Too late, I realized that volunteering to be on the committee with him made it look like I was chasing him. "That's not why I—" I broke off, realizing that there was nothing I could say that would make things better.

Meanwhile, Dino's neck was getting red again.

"I'll be on the committee, too," said a voice from across the room.

A familiar voice: Chloe's.

"Thank you, Ms. Kayson," the teacher said, looking pleased. "A three-person refreshment committee is just perfect."

I looked over at Chloe's hostile face. *Yeah, perfect.*

 **FABFOODZ.COM**

HOME | PROFILE | FRIENDS | RECIPES

Linda Delgado

<u>CLICK</u> FOR MORE PICTURES

RELATIONSHIP STATUS:
Single
INTERESTS: Food, friends,
more food, fun!

What I'm cooking today:
Diet cake. ☹

What else I'm doing: Getting on the
food committee for my school dance
because nobody's gonna ask me

Friends/Family/Foodie Comments:
Fat Foodie says: Can you post the
recipe for the diet cake?
Linda says: It's awful! It's just diet
soda and cake mix.
Julia says: You'll get asked to the
dance, you're a babe!
Linda says: Here in Pittsburgh I'm
a freak!
Julia says: Nope. I won't believe it.

Julia Payette

CLICK FOR MORE PICTURES

RELATIONSHIP STATUS:
Single

INTERESTS: Reading,
computers, cooking. (Yeah,
I'm a geek.)

What I'm cooking today: Real homemade lasagna! Well, it's mostly homemade. We're using those no-boil noodles and already-grated cheese, but at least it doesn't come out of a box like my mom's lasagna! I'll post the recipe after we taste it and tweak it.

What else I'm doing: Hanging with Misty, talking about boys!

Friends/Family/Foodie Comments:
Linda says: That sounds great but . . . I'm jealous.
Julia says: Wish you were here! It smells heavenly.
Linda says: Where RU?
Julia says: Misty's house. Quieter than mine. But . . . I still miss cooking with you and your aunt.
Linda says: Me too!

Chapter Ten

Walmarts are the same everywhere, so walking into one in a suburb of Pittsburgh made me feel right at home.

It was Saturday, and Pat had brought me out on errands with her so we could get a chance to talk. Apparently she took a kid with her each week, and it was my turn.

"Linda," Pat said as we wandered the aisles, throwing canned everything into our shopping cart, "I want to apologize."

"For what?"

"I've been under the weather. I can't seem to shake this little bit of flu, and it's kept me from giving you the help you might need to adjust."

I shrugged. "It's okay."

"No, it's not." Pat shook her head. "I haven't spent as much time with you as I should have. You've been here for three weeks and, aside from a few minutes here and there, we haven't had a chance to sit down and talk about how you're doing."

"I'm okay." It was about half true. I'd gotten used to my

schedule at school, and I'd fixed up my part of the bedroom. I knew my way around.

But I still felt as if there was a big hole in me most of the time. I missed Aunt Elba terribly. And I missed my friends I'd known my whole life.

Trouble was, I didn't know Pat well enough to share my feelings with her.

"How's school going?" she asked. "Are you settling in?"

I nodded. "My classes aren't any harder than back home, except for math. Different books and stuff, but the teachers are helping me catch on."

"How is it sharing a room with Chloe?"

I opened my mouth and shut it again. What could I say? Chloe was a real witch to me most of the time. But she was also Pat's only biological daughter. Pat was going to favor her, obviously; and if I complained about her, I'd make Pat unhappy. "It's going fine," I said.

She eyed me. "She's not being mean?"

Aside from pretending she doesn't know me? I shook my head.

"Well, I'm keeping an eye on that situation," Pat said. She was actually pretty smart; she probably knew I wasn't telling her everything. "I know Chloe can be hard to deal with."

"Thanks," I said.

"Now, there is one other thing I want to talk to you about," she said. "But first, you tell me. What can I do to make life at home better for you? To make you feel more a part of things?"

Pat looked and sounded sincere, so I decided to risk asking for what I truly wanted. "I'd really like to help you cook," I said. "Or even take over a meal a week from you. I could shop for some fresh ingredients, and I'd even clean up—"

Pat held up a hand. "All right, since you mention it, that's what I wanted to discuss with you," she said. "I may not cook the exact foods you're used to, but you've been nothing but negative about the food since you arrived."

"I don't mean to be negative . . ." I trailed off. Was that true? I wanted to cook, but I also wanted to quit eating the gooey, tasteless casseroles that passed for food in Pat's household.

"It feels like you're against the family instead of with us when you complain all the time," she said.

"I'm sorry," I said softly, feeling ashamed. I didn't want to be negative and a complainer. That wasn't how I saw myself. I'd never been that way before. Had my move to Pittsburgh changed me for the worse?

"I help to support the family with *Cooking from Cans*," Pat lectured on. "Do you think it's cheap to raise this many children? That show helps put food on our table."

Bad food, I wanted to say but didn't.

"Let's just declare a moratorium on the subject of meals for a couple of months," she suggested.

I felt my shoulders slump. Two more months of awful food? Two more months banned from the kitchen? "All right," I said, only because I didn't have much of a choice.

She must have read the depression on my face because she picked up the pace. "Come on. We've got time to grab some cheesy nachos on the way out."

"You know, if we stop at the produce section, we could get the stuff to make good nachos at home." I blurted it out before I could stop myself.

She stiffened. "Linda. You don't understand. It's a whole lifestyle. If someone saw me buying all kinds of fresh stuff for my family, I'd be called a hypocrite."

I couldn't keep the skeptical look off my face. "Does anyone really pay that much attention to what you do?"

"Believe me, I have my enemies," she said.

I rolled my eyes. Did she have to be so dramatic? I still couldn't believe that anyone would even watch a stupid show called *Cooking from Cans*.

"I'm tired," she said. "Let's get going, okay?" Her voice was full of reproach. I'd already broken the moratorium, I guess, by mentioning food in a way that could be construed as criticism.

"Sure, whatever."

A lady in a red coat stopped Pat as we were heading to the checkout line. "Excuse me," she said, "but I just had to say hello. You're Pat from the TV show, right?"

Pat smiled and nodded. "Sure am."

"I love, love, love *Cooking from Cans*," she raved. "It's saved me from spending half my day in the kitchen and the other half in the grocery store. I tell you what, I hit Walmart once a month and that's it; I'm done with my shopping."

"Amen, sister." Pat beamed.

"In fact, could you wait while I buy a couple of copies of your cookbook? And sign them for my cousins? They'll make great Christmas gifts."

"Wrap 'em up with a couple of cans of Dinty Moore," Pat suggested. "I'll come over to the book section and sign some copies right now."

"They have your cookbooks here?" I hustled to keep up with Pat, who had delegated the heavy, can-filled grocery cart to me.

She was too busy chatting up her fan to answer; but when we got to the book section, I saw that there were stacks of her books on a big front table, marked down.

Pat pulled out a pen and started signing the books.

"Are you sure it's okay that you do that?" I asked her, looking around to see if anyone from school was in the area. If so, I was definitely going to disappear.

Pat ignored me.

"I can't believe this!" her fan gushed. "I'm so lucky."

A couple of other ladies stopped to see what was going on. Next, a blue-smocked employee came over, had a quick whispered conversation with Pat, and then hurried away. A couple of minutes later, a little table and chair appeared, and there was an announcement over the speaker. "Attention, Walmart shoppers. Pat Kayson, star of *Cooking from Cans*, is signing cookbooks in our book section. So stop on by and find out how you can save time and money while preparing great meals for your family!"

I sat down on the edge of a shelf, kind of hiding behind the shopping cart, thanking Jesus that my last name was different from Pat's.

"Pat, is that your shopping cart?" one of the ladies asked.

"It has to be," said another. "It's nothing but cans. That's amazing!"

Pat didn't look at me, but the "I told you so" vibe rolled off her so thick I could almost smell it.

"Hey, it's not all cans. She's got a few gallons of milk in there," someone else said. "And look at that jumbo pack of ground beef."

"I always say it on my show. Buy meat and milk fresh. Everything else: cans or boxes."

"How many kids are you feeding, Pat?" someone asked.

"Seven," a couple of the women chorused.

"Eight, now," Pat said, gesturing to me. "Linda, here, is the newest addition to our family."

"You're so lucky," a young woman with a couple of runny-nosed toddlers said to me. "Getting to live with a celebrity like Pat. How do you like her cooking?"

Everyone in the small crowd looked at me. I wanted to blurt out my true feelings; but if I did, they'd probably all fry me for lunch.

In Crisco.

"It's like nothing I've ever had before," I compromised. And earned a glare from Pat.

After the silent treatment Pat gave me all the way home in the car, I felt so frustrated that I called Aunt Elba, even though she'd told me not to call unless I really, really needed to talk. But she didn't answer. And she didn't answer the next six times I called her. I even tried texting to no avail.

The more I called without reaching her, the more upset I became. Finally, I summoned up my courage and called my grandparents' land line.

They were the mean, superstrict ones who had ruined Mom's life, who were totally against the fact that I even existed.

My hands shook as I punched numbers into my phone, and when Old Abuela answered, I chickened out and disguised my voice. "May I speak to Elba?" I asked with a southern drawl.

"Elba no está aquí," said my grandmother. "She's in the hospital."

I gasped, panicked, and dropped my disguise. "Grandma, it's Linda. What's the matter with her? Is she okay? Why is she in the hospital?" My black cloud of fear—the one that kicked up whenever I thought about my dead mom and missing dad and how alone I was in the world—rose up inside until I almost choked on it.

Grandma let out a volley of scolding because I hadn't properly introduced myself. She basically called me a liar.

Was it my lucky day for everyone to hate me? But at least my grandmother's harsh words were something to focus on, something besides my fear. "Please just tell me, is Aunt Elba going to be okay?" I asked when I could get a word in.

"She is okay," my grandmother said, her voice softening a

bit. "She is having an operation, and—"

"An operation? For what?"

"It is the surgery of exploration," Old Abuela said. "It is not too serious. The doctors tell us not to worry, and we try to listen. She is healthy, our Elba."

"Thanks," I said, my voice shaky. "Would you . . . would you tell her I called? And let me know if she . . ."

"Of course," Old Abuela said. "Of course we would notify you if her health grows worse."

"Thanks." I clicked off the phone and tried to stop shaking.

Aunt Elba was okay—at least, if Old Abuela was telling me the truth. But I didn't like it that she was in the hospital again. That couldn't mean anything good. Why didn't anyone tell me?

If something happened to her, I'd seriously have to crawl in a hole and die.

I had to face it, though: Aunt Elba was in no position to help with my problems; she had plenty of her own.

There was no escape from my situation here. For now I had to make things work in this family, at this school, in this town.

That was about as cheerful a thought as a burrito made with canned beans.

Linda Delgado

CLICK FOR MORE PICTURES

RELATIONSHIP STATUS:

Single

INTERESTS: Food, friends, more food, fun!

Bad Nachos (Pat Style)

• Open a bag of generic tortilla chips.
• Drizzle on some "pasteurized processed cheese food."
• Garnish with canned jalapeño slices.

Eat. Gag. Feel sick.

Real Nachos (Linda Style)

• Cut yellow corn tortillas into triangles.
• Bake until almost crisp.
• Sauté jalapeños, tomatoes, and onions with garlic and put a spoonful on top of each triangle.
• Top with a cube of good cheese.
• Bake for five more minutes.

Enjoy as a snack or a meal!

That night I couldn't sleep. I went down to the dining room and got on the computer, surfing the FabFoodz site, e-mailing old friends, and looking up pictures of Arizona, which just made me even more homesick.

I couldn't stop worrying. What was going to happen to Aunt Elba? And if something happened to her, what would happen to me?

My pity party got interrupted by the sound of someone crying. At first I thought it was Chloe, but when I tiptoed upstairs to check, our room was quiet.

The sound came from the boys' room, so I opened the door and slid inside. As my eyes adjusted to the darkness, I saw that it was Angel, on his small, temporary cot crowded into a nook beside the dresser.

He was curled into a little ball, sobbing his eyes out but half asleep. The sound was wrenching enough to make me feel like crying, too.

I went over to him and patted his shoulder. "Hey, buddy. You having a nightmare?"

He curled up tighter and cried harder.

And louder. In the bunk beds, I heard Isaiah shifting restlessly.

If he and Sam woke up, the whole house would be in an uproar. Not good, since it was almost 2 a.m. I already knew that Pat got supercranky if she missed out on her sleep.

"Come on." I tried pulling him out of the bed. But he wasn't awake enough to get his feet under himself and walk; he just cried and clutched onto me. So I picked him up and carried him out of the room. Fifty-plus pounds of crying boy was a big load, but I was still pretty strong from all the dish trays I'd lugged around in the restaurant.

I brought him into the living room, climbed into an

overstuffed rocking chair, and held him. "What's wrong?" I asked him in Spanish.

"Mamá, Mamá." Half awake, he cried like his little heart was breaking.

The poor kid. Chloe had told me that his mom had died just a few months before, which was what landed him in foster care. Apparently, she'd come to the US because she'd been alienated from what was left of her family in El Salvador; there were no relatives to take him in. He'd gone to another foster family and had been so unmanageable that they'd booted him out.

Pat had him in counseling, and she and Sir Dad kept him busy and on a schedule. Their rules made all the kids walk a straight line.

But healing from the loss of a mother didn't happen fast. I'd never even known my mother, yet sometimes I felt as if there was a big, empty hole inside me. Losing Aunt Elba just dug that hole deeper.

I held Angel and rocked him and sang a lullaby Aunt Elba still crooned to me sometimes, half joking, when she made me *atolito*, creamed corn soup.

Duérmete, mi niño,
Duérmete solito,
Que cuando despiertes,
Te daré atolito.

Angel settled right down. Maybe it was the familiar tune and words or just the sound of Spanish, or maybe it was the rocking.

I heard something in the house, someone getting up to go to the bathroom probably, and stopped singing. But Angel started to fuss again, so I cuddled him closer and sang again quietly.

Suddenly I realized: he needed me. No one else in this family did. I was used to being needed in the restaurant, and I could see now that that was part of my problem here. I wasn't accustomed to being a regular kid; I felt better if someone depended on me.

This sweet little jerk was tugging at my heart. I ate it up.

Until Pat came out in her bathrobe and flipped on a light. "What're you doing up?" she asked in an irritated voice.

Angel started to cry, loudly this time.

"Turn off the light," I snapped. "I just got him calmed down."

"Mamá," Angel wailed.

Pat shook her head and held out her arms. "I'll take over."

"He was fine until you came in." I wanted to add, *He wants his real mother, not you*; but it seemed too mean, so I bit back the comment.

Angel cried harder.

"Linda, I don't have the energy for this argument right now. Please, just go to bed."

"Fine." I stood up, dumped Angel into her arms, and stomped off to my bedroom. Why couldn't she ever let me help? Why couldn't she ever see anything I did as good enough?

My only satisfaction was that Angel's crying went on long into the night. I cried, too, for a little while, wondering how long I was destined to stay in Pat's alien family.

When I finally got Aunt Elba on the phone the next day, I couldn't help asking, "Don't you want me to come take care of you?"

"No, no. That is the last thing I'd want for you." I heard her slightly labored breathing. "I'm sorry I didn't tell you and Pat about my little operation. I didn't want you to worry."

"I worried more because I didn't know what was going on!" I scolded her. "Promise me you won't keep secrets anymore."

"If I have to go to the hospital, I will tell you and Pat," she said. "But meanwhile, it's good for you there, isn't it? You are learning how to live in a family?"

Her voice sounded so hopeful that I heard myself saying things were fine. I didn't want to upset her. Here I'd just gotten her to promise to be honest, and I was lying myself! "I'll talk to you when you feel better," I told her.

But when I hung up the phone, I knew I had my answer for real this time: I had to stay here, and I *had* to make it work.

Chapter Eleven

"Nick DeLuca is coming here?" Chloe jumped up from the kitchen table.

It was Wednesday afternoon, and we'd been doing homework in fairly companionable silence. Our room was a little cramped and chilly, but the kitchen was warm since Pat had a casserole baking in the oven. Tonight was tuna and noodles.

"Is that a problem?" I asked her as she gathered up her books. "The math teacher assigned him to me as a tutor. He seems okay for a numbers genius."

"And you didn't know he's Dino Moretti's cousin?"

"No way!"

My shock must have convinced her that I wasn't scheming to get Dino through this guy, because she allowed herself a small smile. "Yeah, polar opposites, right? Nick's a desperate and dateless dweeb."

"He's on the football team. He told me."

"Parks and Rec, and they let anyone join," she informed me. "And why is he coming here, anyway? Why isn't he meeting you at school like all the other tutors do?"

I shrugged. "He asked if we could meet at my house, and I said it was fine."

"And then he got all excited, right?"

I propped my elbows on my math book and rested my chin on my folded hands, thinking about it. "Yeah. Actually, he did," I said, surprised.

She rolled her eyes. "He so thinks he's going to get it on with you." She picked up a handful of mechanical pencils as the front doorbell rang.

I jumped up and grabbed her by the arm. "You can't leave. You have to help me!"

She laughed. "Oh, no. You got yourself into this."

"But I didn't know."

"And he's counting on that."

"But he's, like, six feet tall and two hundred pounds," I said. "What if he tackles me? Your mom's not even here."

"You should have thought of that before you invited him to our house," she said heartlessly, and clomped off toward the stairs in her combat boots.

I wove my way through action figures and game consoles to the front door, planning my strategy. I could stand up to this. I didn't need to get intimidated by a boy. Jeez, I'd fended off four drunk adults at a time working in the restaurant.

Thinking of that made me smile with a weird sort of nostalgia. I didn't miss fending off drunk guys, but I missed the diss sessions with Aunt Elba afterward.

I opened the door to find Nick DeLuca there, math book and calculator in hand. He pushed his way in before I even had a chance to greet him, but I could see why. Angel, Sam, and Isaiah had shot him with their water guns. His jeans and jacket were half soaked, and he was shivering.

"Get lost," I yelled at them. Then I realized I'd just dismissed my front line of defense. "Come into the kitchen," I said to Nick, who was attempting to look cool while wiping his face on his sleeve. "You want a dish towel?"

He accepted the towel and dried himself off as best he could, blushing. I couldn't help giggling when I realized that the boys had soaked him in an embarrassing place.

I pressed my advantage. "So, Nick, I hear it's not usual for tutors to meet students at home. Any particular reason you wanted to?"

"Well, I, uh—"

"If you thought it would be more convenient, I guess you just figured out you were wrong." I looked pointedly at his water-stained jeans.

His fair skin made him unable to hide his flaming blush. "What's that smell?" he blurted out.

"It's my aunt's delicious tuna-noodle casserole; and trust me, the smell gets stronger as it cooks." I sat down at the table. "Ready to tutor me?"

The poor guy was completely off his game, so I showed him my homework and exactly what I didn't understand, and he explained it to me. Like six times! I couldn't believe how far behind I was in math. I guess my Arizona school district didn't follow the same curriculum, or maybe I was dumber than I thought.

Nick was actually pretty helpful. Halfway through our session, Chloe came down and was a total witch to him. A little later Pat came home and ran the electric can opener a bunch of times, opening giant cans of green beans to go along with the casserole, which had lived up to my prediction and started to truly reek.

In this house, that can opener sound brought all the boys into the kitchen like a crowd of hungry cats. Now they were dressed up in their new Halloween costumes—a wrestler, a skeleton, and a zombie complete with fake blood—and they whooped and hollered around the table.

"Can we go to your room?" Nick asked, his voice hopeless like he knew what a feeble chance he had.

"Chloe's there," I said, smiling blandly at him. "But it might be a good idea to meet at school next time, huh?"

He nodded and stood up, looking defeated. "Yeah."

"We're getting ready to have dinner," Pat said over her shoulder to Nick as she pulled the giant tuna-noodle casserole out of the oven. "You're welcome to stay. There's plenty." As a visual aid, she held the foul-smelling casserole toward him.

"Um, no thanks," he said, taking a step back and running into the table. He turned and started scooping up his books. "Linda, I gotta go home."

"Thanks for all the help," I said, meaning it. "If my family hasn't scared you off, can we set up an appointment for next week?"

"Sure, just check my schedule in the tutoring lab and sign up for a slot. That's how we usually do it." He was already in the kitchen doorway.

I followed him to the front door. He was actually a nice guy, and I felt kind of sorry for him. "Thanks for making a house call this first time," I said, trying not to smile.

"Right. Later."

As I shut the door behind him, I let my grin come to the surface. Every now and then it was all right to have a big, crazy family.

Linda Delgado

CLICK FOR MORE PICTURES

RELATIONSHIP STATUS:
Single

INTERESTS: Food, friends, more food, fun!

What I'm cooking today: Nothing, again ☹

What else I'm doing: Finding new uses for bad food! Check out the photo of tuna-noodle casserole that I used to scare away a hottie-in-his-own-mind.

Friends/Family/Foodie Comments:

Julia says: What did you do—throw it at him? Feed it to him?

Linda says: The odor alone did the trick—he ran.

Fish Fan says: I have a personal crusade to eliminate tuna-noodle casserole from the universe! Who's still cooking it?

Linda says: Tune in to Cooking from Cans if you're in the Pittsburgh area.

Fat Foodie: Hey, I watch that show for a laugh sometimes. But why'd you cook TNC if you hate it?

> **Linda says:** Not my choice.
> I have the privilege of living
> with the ultimate cooker-
> from-cans.
> **Mom2Nine says:** OMG, I
> love that show! Pat's a hoot.

Most of the time, the big family and the bad food made me desperate to escape. And thanks to the food section of the Pittsburgh paper, I figured out how: the Strip District, Pittsburgh's downtown, open-air market. The next Saturday, I told Pat and Sir Dad that I was headed for the public library and then braved the city bus to get there.

It was November now. Most of the trees had shed their leaves, which blew around the streets in the windy sunshine. Peppers, garlic, and onions hung from the ceilings of multiple stalls; and bins of pumpkins and winter squash lined the street. From a giant open-air shop, fresh fish emitted its pungent aroma.

Even though it was chilly, plenty of Pittsburghers were out. Street vendors sold everything from jewelry to T-shirts to used books, and a guy blew up balloons and shaped them into animals for families who passed by. A woman played her violin next to an open case that held a few dollars, quarters, and even pennies from the cheap at heart.

Being from the rural part of Arizona, I'd never seen anything like it. The closest thing was a market I'd visited in a Mexican border town, but this was much bigger. Plus, it was mostly focused on food.

I followed my nose to a bakery stand, picked out what I wanted from the bins, and got in line to pay.

I was glad I'd come. I told myself I was buying a few samples to get ideas for the refreshments at First Formal, but the truth was that if I didn't get out of bad-canned-food land soon, I'd go completely *loco*!

Here were people who understood that fresh was better than canned. Here were shoppers who visited a special market to get the very best. My people.

Of course, there were other kinds of people, too. Like the salesman with the leather-studded T-shirt standing behind a table stacked high with merchandise. He looked somewhat familiar.

And then I saw someone else who looked *very* familiar, someone I didn't expect to see down here in food land.

Dino!

He was pushing and shoving the T-shirt guy, who, I now realized, was my math tutor . . . only dressed like no math tutor I'd ever seen before.

I was so mesmerized by the scene that the person in line behind me cleared his throat. At which point I realized that the line was moving, and I scuttled ahead. In my hand were the samples of biscotti and napoleons that I thought we could use as models for some really special refreshments for the fall dance. I just had to pay for them.

"Hey, Linda, what're you doing down here?" came Nick's voice.

I turned back around in time to see Dino trying to shush Nick. Then he got very busy doing something on the ground behind the table.

He was trying to hide from me!

"Don't you recognize me?" Nick called again. "From school!"

Then he stumbled against the table. Obviously, Dino had grabbed his leg and tried to trip him. Oh, that was too much.

"Hi, Nick," I called, waving in a superfriendly way. "Who's

your friend down there on the ground?"

People in line were starting to stare at me. Luckily, I was next. But the woman in front of me had two little kids who kept running around, so she was taking forever.

"I'll be right over," I sang out. "Don't go away!"

Chapter Twelve

When I got over to the T-shirt table with my bag of pastries, Dino was there. With a scowl on his face.

"What are you doing down here by yourself?" he asked, his tone suggesting I'd committed some kind of a crime. "Where's your family?"

"I escaped them," I said. "What about you guys? What're you doing here?"

Nick gave me a huge smile. He was a little bit like a St. Bernard puppy, so big and eager that you just wanted to pet him. "I run this T-shirt business on the weekends," he explained.

"Are you old enough to have your own business?" Now that I looked more closely at the T-shirts, I saw that most of them were math related. "And does anyone buy them?"

"No, I'm not old enough, but I get away with it by calling it a school project. And yes, of course people buy them! Lots of people like math."

"Lots of parents *want* their kids to like math and buy them T-shirts," Dino corrected.

"And for you, milady, I have zee free shirt," Nick said in an accent meant to be funny. "Zis shirt vill help you ace your next math test." He held up a pink shirt with some math formula on it. "It's the Pythagorean theorem," he added shyly in his normal voice.

"Gosh, I don't know what to say." I took it, biting my lip to keep from giggling. "Thank you, Nick."

Dino caught my eye, and something sparked between us. He thought it was funny, too, but had chosen not to laugh, just like me.

"If I could leave my work station, I'd take you out for zee coffee," Nick said, getting back to the sort-of-funny accent. "But, alas, all my merchandise will be stolen—and *poof*! There will go my college fund."

"Too bad." I smiled at him. I actually liked this version of Nick. He seemed relaxed down here. All this good food made people much more authentic.

"I'll buy you some coffee," Dino said suddenly. "Um, I mean, if you need a caffeine fix."

I raised an eyebrow at him. "I wouldn't want to put you out."

"No, I want to."

"Hey." Nick put a lot of unhappiness into that little word.

"We have to work together on food for the dance committee," I told him. "It'll be a working date." Then I felt myself blush all the way up to my eyeballs. Who'd said anything about a date?

"Come on," Dino said, and pulled me away.

I couldn't even answer him back. Because he kept on holding my hand, and the warm feel of it somehow erased the words from my brain.

"Thanks for rescuing me," I managed finally. "You didn't have to, but I'm glad you did."

"I've been kind of a jerk to you," he admitted, which surprised me.

We walked a half block through the crowd, with him pulling me along by the hand. Finally we came to a less crowded spot. "So what are you doing down here?" I asked him.

"Just hanging around." He didn't look at me.

"Hanging around doing what?"

He dropped my hand. "Nothing."

Now that was interesting. Dino was hiding something. "So what's the big secret, huh?" I teased. "Do you have a girlfriend down here or something? You can tell me; I won't spread the word."

He laughed, looking embarrassed. "It's not a girlfriend."

"Then what?" I persisted.

"Nothing," he said. "Nothing!"

"All right, I'll stop bugging you. But I know you've got a secret."

He rolled his eyes, but he didn't look completely upset to have me teasing him.

We strolled on through the stalls together. I inhaled the scent of freshly ground coffee beans, ran my hands over rough-skinned squash, and examined jars of new-to-me spices. Dino didn't say much, but he looked at stuff with me and acted more interested than most guys would have. He was dressed in an old T-shirt and jeans; and just like his cousin, he seemed more relaxed here than at school. We were actually having fun together.

"Hey, Moretti!" called a voice, and we both glanced over to see a teenage street musician waving his sax at us. "You finally got a girlfriend?"

Really quickly I looked at Dino's face. Red as a tomato.

What did that mean? Was the idea of me as a girlfriend so awful to him? Or maybe, just maybe, was he thinking of me that way?

An old man passing out samples of Cuban sandwiches in front of his shop picked up the teasing. "Young Dino! About time you found a pretty girl!"

I didn't know what to say, and neither did Dino, apparently; he was blushing and shaking his head at them. He looked as if he didn't know whether to laugh or get mad.

"How come they all know you?" I asked. "Do you come down here a lot? It's a long way from our neighborhood."

Just then another guy called out some comment.

"Let's get off the street," Dino said, looking around. He tugged me toward a little pastry shop. "Want a pastry?"

I was too hyper to be hungry, but I was curious to learn more about Dino. So I nodded. "Sure, okay."

He took my hand again to lead me inside. He ordered us a couple of pastries and hot chocolate and then led me to a table in the back of the shop hidden from the front and sheltered by some tall plants.

Was he trying to hide from people? Or was he trying to get romantic?

I scolded myself for being a silly girl. Dino hadn't asked me out or anything. He was a popular, show-offy kid who had just happened to run into me on a Saturday. He'd taken pity on the new girl, but that was no reason to think he was falling in love with me.

He pushed one of the pastries toward me. "Here, try this one. Look out, it's not exactly sweet."

I took a bite and my eyes widened. "That's fantastic!" I exclaimed, then blushed because I was talking with my mouth full. The flaky pastry held a savory meat blend with just a touch of sweet flavor.

He grinned. "I figured you'd like it."

I swallowed and wiped my mouth. "Oregano, cilantro, and a little . . . nutmeg, I think," I said.

"Really?" He took my hand and guided the pastry to his mouth, and took a bite. He kept on holding my hand, with the pastry in it, while he chewed. "I'm thinking ginger, not nutmeg."

"No way." I took another bite. "I know it's not ginger. But maybe . . . cloves?"

"That's it!" He grinned. "You're good. How'd you learn so much about cooking?"

So I told him all about Aunt Elba and the restaurant. That led to a bunch of questions about life in Arizona, and speaking Spanish, and why I'd moved to Pennsylvania. Dino was a good listener—he kept asking more questions whenever I stopped talking—so I basically spilled my whole life story.

"So now wait a minute," he said when I paused for breath. "You moved in with Pat Kayson. The famous *Cooking from Cans* lady."

"That's right." I started to say how much I hated her food, but I stopped myself. There was this thing called family loyalty, and right then I felt a little bit of it toward Pat.

"Then you live with scary Chloe, right?"

I clapped my hand over my mouth. "Oh, no!" Talk about loyalty issues. "Chloe would kill me if she knew you knew. I'm not supposed to let anyone know I'm part of her family now."

"Your secret is safe with me," he said, giving my arm a quick rub. I felt it all the way to my toes! "Now, tell me about this FabFoodz page."

So I did. Julia had started adding a lot of fun recipes; and because our pages were linked, we were getting more visitors. Dino said he'd check it out the next time he was online, leading me to look back and wonder if I'd posted anything embarrassing. Well, I had put up that thing about scaring Nick away with the tuna-noodle casserole, but that was okay for Dino to see.

A couple of times I tried to turn the conversation around by asking him about his family. But unlike most boys, he didn't seem to enjoy talking about himself. He dodged my questions and spun the dialogue back my way.

We'd moved on into analyzing our teachers when a big man with gray-and-black streaked hair and a dirty apron over his enormous belly barreled into the pastry shop and stood, hands on hips. "I'm looking for my no-good son," he blared.

Something in the man's voice made me think of Dino. I turned to look at him.

Dino slumped back onto the wall like he was trying to blend in with it. But he had no such luck, because the lady behind the counter nodded his way.

The giant man stumped back. "I look all up and down this street for you," he said with a thick accent, probably Italian. His hands waved up and down to emphasize his words. "My young son of leisure. Too busy flirting and eating sweets at someone else's shop to help his father out on the busiest day of the week!"

Dino shrank down farther in his chair. He didn't look at me.

"Playing the rich boy," his father raved on. He glanced around, saw he had an audience, and started waving his hands even more dramatically. "This one wants to be president of the United States. This one is too good to dirty his hands with the work that puts food in his mouth."

I couldn't help feeling sorry for Dino. Everyone in the shop was watching the scene. A well-dressed couple tried to conceal their laughter. Meanwhile, behind the counter, the workers just rolled their eyes and shook their heads, as if this was an argument they'd heard before.

"I'm coming, Dad," Dino said when his father finally stopped for breath. He got up from his chair. "Sorry," he muttered to me, his face red and mortified, and started to slink away.

"We are almost out of olive salad," his father was saying as Dino followed him. "Other work the hired help can do, but our recipes stay in the family."

I stared at the two of them as a bunch of things came together for me. Dino smelled good all the time, like oregano and garlic and basil. He must do the cooking in his family's shop, or grocery, or whatever it was. But he was flunking cooking class—what was that all about? Did he worry that if he cooked at school, everyone would know that he cooked for a living?

Anyway, what was so bad about that?

All of a sudden Dino's dad stopped, turned around, and looked at me. "Did you pay for her food?"

"I got it, Dad." And then they left the pastry shop, leaving me to pick at my pastry and wonder why Dino pretended to be something he wasn't.

Linda Delgado

CLICK FOR MORE PICTURES

RELATIONSHIP STATUS:
Single

INTERESTS: Food, friends, more food, fun!

A shout-out to Pittsburgh's Strip District, where you can buy:
• Fresh peppers, cilantro, and parsley
• Meat pastries to die for
• Fish so fresh it can practically swim (yes, Pat, there is fish that doesn't come from cans)
• Math-related T-shirts! Yeah, I got one. But it was a gift.

Friends/Family/Foodie Comments:
Julia says: Sounds like someone had a fun weekend! Hey, check out my fry bread recipe. It'll make you homesick! Miss you!

Julia Payette

<u>CLICK</u> FOR MORE PICTURES

RELATIONSHIP STATUS:

Single

INTERESTS: Reading, computers, cooking. (Yeah, I'm a geek.)

What I'm cooking today:

My Navajo Granny's
Indian Fry Bread

Ingredients:
1 cup flour
Pinch of salt
2 pinches baking powder
Handful powdered milk
½ cup warm water

• Combine quickly and lightly—don't knead it to death! Make a ball and flatten until it's like a plate. Cut the flat dough into four pieces.
• Heat an inch of oil in a frying pan until a little ball of dough sizzles in it, then fry your dough one piece at a time, 3–4 minutes on each side.
• Serve hot with powdered sugar or jam, or use like a taco shell.

Friends/Family/Foodie Comments:
Misty says: Heavy on the oil, isn't it?

Linda says: Yeah, and isn't it kind of plain?

Julia says: Hey, when you're eating government-issued food on the rez, you use what you've got! Have a heart for the recipe's history, girls!

Linda says: Sorry, my bad. Props to Granny, always. And I do remember it being delicious!

Chapter Thirteen

The next Monday in cooking class, our teacher made us give a progress report on the dance refreshments.

"There is no progress," Dino said, earning a laugh from his buddies.

Dino was back to acting like he'd never get his hands dirty working in a restaurant—and like he barely knew me. I kept wondering if I'd dreamed our encounter on Saturday.

"That won't do," our teacher said. "You three take over Kitchen Seven and have a meeting. You need to get started."

Chloe, Dino, and I gathered our stuff and headed for Kitchen Seven, right next to Kitchen Six, where Mindy and Mandy complained about having to work alone. This was mainly for Dino's benefit. Both of them openly flirted with him. He flirted back, too, a little. The rat.

As we sat down at the table, my brain went into overdrive, trying to sort things out. Chloe liked Dino, of course. And she wanted to stop me from having any kind of friendship with him. Because of that, I hadn't told her about meeting him in the

Strip District, let alone that his family had a shop there.

Secret #1.

Chloe's secret was that she didn't want anyone to know we were related and living together. From watching her with Sir Dad and playing amateur psychologist, I'd guessed that she wished she was his only child, didn't want to share him, and felt that if her parents had loved her enough, they wouldn't have had to adopt all those other kids. Another girl in the family, her exact same age, was too much of a threat. Plus, apparently she sometimes got teased about all her different-looking siblings; and being a sensitive poet type, she couldn't handle the heat.

So the fact that we were living under one roof was secret #2.

Secret #3 was the fact that Chloe didn't know that Dino knew secret #2, thanks to my big mouth.

It made sitting at a small table together pretty difficult.

"So, um, what are we going to make for refreshments?" I asked, trying to get the meeting over with as soon as possible.

Dino shrugged. "Doesn't matter."

That annoyed me. "Oh, no, you don't," I said. "You're not leaving all the planning and work to us just because you're a guy. I happen to know you can cook."

Dino turned red, but didn't say anything.

Chloe rushed to his defense. "How would you know that?" she asked me sharply. "Is it because of your weird thing about smells? Did it ever occur to you that maybe his mom's a good cook—"

"Unlike *your* mom," I said.

"Hey." She kicked me, hard, under the table.

"Ow!" I reached down to rub my shin. "Anyway, does anyone have any ideas about refreshments? Because I do if you don't."

"Go for it," Dino said.

Chloe crossed her arms and glared at me.

I took a deep breath. "Okay. Well, I tried a bunch of food

when I went down to the Strip District on Saturday. And I think we should go for two main kinds. First, fresh fruit like pineapple and strawberries, because the girls won't want anything fattening." I glanced over at Mandy and Mindy. "If we cut them up and use toothpicks, it won't get all over their dresses."

"Makes sense," Chloe said with reluctant respect.

"And it won't take too much time," Dino added.

"The second kind," I said, "should be a meat-filled pastry." I looked at Dino. "Like that one we tried at the bakery, you know?" Then I clapped my hand over my mouth.

Secret #1 was almost out.

"When did you guys try pastry?" Chloe asked suspiciously.

I looked at Dino.

He looked at the table.

"We ran into each other down in the Strip District on Saturday," I said.

Chloe reeled back and stared at Dino. "I know *she's* into food, but what were *you* doing in the Strip?"

"I get around," he said, scraping with his fingernail at some dried batter or something left on the table by another class.

Chloe put both hands on the table and leaned forward. "Are you two dating?"

"Would that be a crime?" Dino asked.

At the same moment, I said, "No! He works at his family's shop down there, that's all."

Then Dino and I stared at each other.

Heat came into my face as I realized what he'd said. *Would that be a crime? Did he want* to date me?

But his face pulled up into a frown. "Do you have to spill all my secrets?" he asked me.

"Your family's shop?" Chloe asked in a loud, upset voice. Clearly, she was jealous that I knew more about Dino than she did.

I put my hand over her mouth. "Don't broadcast it, okay, cousin? Or should I call you Roomie?"

Dino looked from me to Chloe.

Chloe gave me a dirty look. "Thanks a lot," she said. "Talk about broadcasting."

"Whatever." Why did I always have to be the one to watch what I said? "It's not like I'm crazy about living in Canned Food Heaven."

"Hey, Chloe," said a voice behind us. I turned around to see that Mandy and Mindy were unabashedly eavesdropping from Kitchen Six. "Don't you have, like, seven or eight brothers and sisters already?"

Chloe's face took on a new shade of fuchsia. It was not her best color.

"Seven," I answered, because she wasn't going to.

"God, what are your parents doing? Trying to make their own little rainbow coalition?"

Chloe turned to me, her nostrils flaring and her eyes flinty. "Now look what you did. Everyone in school is gonna know about this within an hour."

I parked my hands on my hips. "What's the big deal? They already seem to know. Why would anyone care?"

"The gossip mill around here is vicious," she said. "And those two are at the center of it."

Dino slumped forward, shoulders bowed. "Wonder if they heard about my family, too?"

Chloe saw her chance to bond with him—against me—and went for it. "You've sure run off your mouth today, Linda," she said. "Don't worry, Dino. I won't tell anyone."

All of a sudden I found myself on my feet, hands on hips again, heart pounding. "I don't know what your problem is," I yelled at them. "You both act like your families are something to be ashamed of. But you both have a mom and a dad, and a home, and food on the table. Did it ever occur to you that those are things to be thankful for? Did you ever realize there are people who don't have any of those things?"

Chloe stared at me, her mouth hanging open. Dino looked like he was about to argue, but nothing came out. Around us, the room was eerily quiet. When I grabbed my notebook and spun around, I realized that everyone in the class, including the teacher, was staring at me. They must have heard every word I'd said.

So much for secrets.

And so much for refreshments for First Formal.

"Look," I said to Dino and Chloe, "I'll bring the recipes for those foods to our next class. If you have a better idea, you bring it. Otherwise, we'll cook what I say." I paused, then added, "Got it?"

They both nodded, staring at me. I glanced at the teacher, who was smiling just a little, and took the risk of walking out of class.

The next day I pretended to be sick so I could get a break from all the gossip and tension at school. When I woke up again at 11 a.m. I was starving, so I crept downstairs to see if I could find some food.

Voices were coming from the kitchen. Familiar voices. Pat and Mrs. Piotrowski. I heard my name and sat on the bottom step to eavesdrop.

"Linda is a help with him, but he's still quite difficult," Pat was saying. "He wakes up in the night a lot. He's grieving the loss of his mother. But he's also angry about all that's happened to him, and his way of expressing anger is to lash out physically."

So Pat did pay attention to Angel, and apparently, the night I'd heard him crying wasn't the first time it had happened.

"We've got him in counseling, and on consistent rules, but progress is slow."

"Do you think you'll keep him?" Mrs. Piotrowski asked.

I heard clattering cups and the sound of coffee being poured, and I leaned closer, trying to hear.

"I don't know," Pat said finally. "I'm not one to give up on a child, you know that. But we really don't have the space; and right now, I don't seem to have the energy I used to have. Maybe I'm getting too old for this."

The voices murmured on while I thought about Angel. What would happen to him if Pat kicked him out? Would he go to a family where there was no one who spoke Spanish? Would he get even more hurt and hostile?

"...adopt him," Pat was saying. "I guess there are a few more distant relatives to check on, but no one from his family down in El Salvador has come forward to take him in. If he's declared free for adoption, we'll have to either say we want him permanently, or his dossier and photo will go out on the national Adoption Exchange."

"Along with thousands of other children, right?"

"Unfortunately, that's right. The odds of finding a permanent family aren't all that great for a little boy with his issues."

"What about Linda? Is she staying?"

I rose silently to my feet and tiptoed closer to hear Pat's answer.

"Well, that's another question," she said. "Her aunt is ill and can't take care of her now, and we don't know whether that's a temporary situation or permanent."

"She's a lovely girl," Mrs. P said.

"She can be," Pat agreed with hesitation in her voice.

What was that supposed to mean?

"I know you have to get to the studio, dear, but it's been so nice to chat with you," Mrs. Piotrowski said. The sound of scraping chairs made me bolt halfway back up the stairs. "If you ever need anything for any of these kids, you can call on me."

I backed farther up the stairs so they wouldn't see me as Pat escorted Mrs. P to the door. I didn't feel like seeing either of them.

Poor Angel. Poor me. I was worried about both of us.

But as I sat on my bed flipping through my old cookbooks for comfort, an idea came to me.

Pat obviously didn't think I was much of a help around the house. And I guess I wasn't, but that was because she wouldn't let me.

Meanwhile, she'd said she was getting old and didn't have enough energy for Angel.

All Pat needed to do, it seemed to me, was to get over her block against my cooking, and it would be a win for everyone: me, Pat, and Angel.

And I knew the perfect place to ask her.

Chapter Fourteen

"You're sure you want to confront Mom at work?" Jen asked as she pulled up to a building marked CHANNEL EIGHT in big, looping letters. When Jen mentioned that she had to run some errands, including picking up Pat at the local television studio where *Cooking from Cans* was produced, I'd jumped on it. Angel was with us, too, since Sir Dad needed the quiet. "She gets pretty focused here," Jen continued. "I usually wait for her in the car."

"What better place to confront the chef than in her kitchen?" Pat was professional, and positive, and in a good mood here, or at least that was how she seemed when I'd watched episodes of her show. As I looked at the building, though, I felt uneasy. "This place is sort of dingy looking."

"Yeah, the station's going through budget cuts. In fact, they let the receptionist go last month, but you should still wait by the front desk. Don't bother Mom in the studio." Jen patted my shoulder. "I'll be back as soon as I pick up Angel's meds."

"I go with Linda," Angel said from the backseat.

"No, Angel." Jen still couldn't pronounce his name right,

even though I'd explained it to the family. "Mama Pat's very busy in there. It's no place for little kids."

"*Hay una niña.*" Angel pointed at a mother, father, and blond girl who looked about Angel's age walking into the studio. "Hey, Samantha!" he yelled out the door at the girl.

"You know her?" I asked Angel. Then I turned to Jen. "Maybe he can play with her. I don't mind taking Angel with me." I emphasized my correct pronunciation of his name: *ahn-hell*. Truthfully, ever since Angel had needed me in the night, I'd felt a bond with him. That had grown stronger when I'd heard Pat discussing his future with Mrs. P.

Jen narrowed her eyes at the family. "If they'll let anyone play with their little foodie princess."

Well, well, well. Perky Jen had a grudge against someone.

"He'll be fine," I assured her.

"Are you sure you can make him behave?"

"Piece of cake. C'mon, Angel."

We got inside just in time to see the family disappear into a room marked STUDIO THREE.

"*¡Vamos!*" Angel said.

I grabbed him by the shoulders. "We can go in if you'll be totally quiet."

"*Sí, sí,*" he agreed with his sweet smile.

When we slipped into the audience area of the recording studio, there was Pat. Her TV makeup had turned her into a clown version of herself. She was superpeppy in a clownlike way, too.

"What's the problem with canned stew? Not enough meat, right? So here"—she held up a jumbo package of beef already cut into chunks—"we solve the problem. Just dump the meat and the canned stew into Mom's best friend, the Crock-Pot, and you're off duty for the rest of the day."

I was fascinated in a sick way. I'd sometimes imagined having my own cooking show, so it was cool to see the TV kitchen up there under the lights, with its fancy sink and shining stovetop and beautiful golden wood cupboards.

"Sit down and watch Mama Pat," I told Angel. I punched in Julia's number and got her at home, a small miracle. The girl was one of about eighteen in America who didn't have a cell phone; plus she babysat and helped in the school's homework lab to earn extra cash. After we'd gushed at each other about how long it had been since we talked, I told her what was going on. "This great kitchen is so wasted on Pat," I explained. "She's making double-meat Dinty Moore. Oh, wait. Now she's slapping canned biscuits on a baking sheet. I'm so sure."

"You should try to be on TV," Julia said. "Maybe this is your chance!"

"I'd rather die than be on her show," I said, then lowered my voice when I realized that there were a couple of people near me in the back of the shadowy studio. "Listen, I'd better go."

The family we'd seen walking in earlier edged toward me, and I started to panic. Were they Pat's spies, and had they overheard me talking trash about her?

"Hey," said the woman. "I'm Leslie, and this is Trevor. And this is our daughter, Samantha."

I looked around for Angel to introduce him, but he wasn't in sight. A twinge of uneasiness worked its way through my stomach, but I flashed a friendly smile.

"We're up next," Trevor explained. "Channel Eight films both of its cooking shows on one day. Are you auditioning to be on Pat's show?"

"Not exactly," I said. "I'm . . . not a fan."

"Oh, God, neither are we," Leslie said. "What's she making today?"

"Canned stew with extra prechopped meat thrown in it," I

said, keeping my tone neutral. Then I couldn't help it: I started giggling.

Leslie laughed, too, and Trevor rolled his eyes. "She is un-effing-believable," he said.

"You mean you guys cook fresh? On your show?"

"Only fresh. We're like the polar opposite of Pat, and the network is measuring viewer appeal for both shows. We heard that a syndication rep will be out here any day now to make a decision about which show to request."

"No way."

"Way. We thought you might be that person, from the back."

"Right, and then you realized I'm fourteen."

"But fourteen with good taste," Trevor said. "The day she put canned asparagus on top of Spam and squirted it with Cheez Whiz, we thought we'd die."

I couldn't help making a face.

"Yeah, and what did she call that day's show? 'Canned Foods with Class' or something?"

When Leslie and Trevor learned that I lived with Pat, they were full of sympathy, and pressed me for more horror stories. Pretty soon we were all laughing and bringing up examples of Pat's bad food. I felt a little guilty, but mostly I was glad to find people who understood what I went through on a daily basis. We were careful, too: we watched to make sure that Pat didn't overhear us. She was up front having a talk with some man in a suit and hadn't yet realized I was even there.

I ended up telling Leslie and Trevor about my FabFoodz page, figuring they were the type to know about the site. Sure enough, they did.

"You know Pat's on it, too, right?" Leslie asked.

"She *is*?" Uneasy, I thought back over what I'd written. It wasn't exactly flattering to Pat and her show.

But she'd never visit a teen's page. Would she?

When Pat's discussion ended, Leslie and Trevor went up toward the kitchen. I was about to head up, too, when I felt a hand on my shoulder.

It was Jen. "Where's Angel?"

I looked around. To be honest, I'd forgotten all about him, but I was relieved to see him sitting beside Samantha playing rock, paper, scissors. I pointed, and Jen raised her eyebrows. But she had more important things to scold me about. "Why were you talking to those guys?" she wanted to know.

"Just a little foodie fun." I wondered how much she'd overheard.

"Well, stay away from them. They're Mom's competitors with the syndication service. Only one cooking show from Pittsburgh is likely to go nationwide, and they'll do anything to beat out Mom."

Her words made me feel crawly inside, like I'd betrayed a trust. Like, heck: I *had* betrayed Pat. When I looked up front and saw Leslie and Trevor smiling and gushing to Pat, acting like her best friends, I had to question why they'd been so nice to me. They were probably laughing at me behind my back, too.

Jen and I approached the studio kitchen in time to hear Trevor ask, "Pat, are you going to use that new comp cookware?"

She shook her head. "Doubt it. You two want it?" She held out a set of pans Aunt Elba would have died for.

"Are you sure?" Leslie took the pans and touched them reverently. Her eyes met Trevor's, and he winked as if to say, *She's such an idiot.*

I felt even more crawly inside then. Was I like Leslie and Trevor? Suddenly, I didn't want to be.

"What are you doing here?" Pat asked when she spotted Jen and me.

"Linda wanted to see—" Jen started to say.

At that moment Samantha came running to her mother at full speed. "Mommy! He hit me!"

Leslie immediately scooped her up. "Are you okay, honey?"

"He's a bad boy," she said, pointing to Angel from her safe perch in her mother's arms. "The teacher says so, too. He got his name on the board five times in one day!"

I heard a growl behind me. Angel. Uh-oh.

I turned to grab him, but it was too late.

He latched onto Leslie's leg like one of those magnetic cling monkeys and started punching and scratching her. A volley of curse words—worthy of any trucker I'd heard in the diner, but thankfully in Spanish—spewed from his mouth.

"Ow! Get him off me!" Leslie howled, and shook her leg, clad in expensive, thin stockings that were definitely history.

Pat, Jen, and I all dived for Angel.

Angel started thrashing and howling, and Jen wrapped her arms and legs around him from behind, holding him down.

"Who," Pat gritted out between his screams, "brought him in here?"

Jen didn't say anything, but her eyes darted toward me.

Samantha was transfixed by the scene, and Trevor had squatted down to examine Leslie's leg. "The skin's not broken," he said with distaste, "but it's definitely going to bruise."

Then Angel got loose from Jen and started running around the studio, knocking things over. "Get that on film!" Trevor ordered the cameragirl.

"C'mon, Linda, we have to get him!" Jen was scrambling to her feet.

"Leslie, I'm so sorry," Pat said. "I take responsibility. My kids should know better than to bring a little one in here."

"Well, some little ones can handle it, but *yours* obviously can't."

I wanted to chime in; but Jen was having a hard time

cornering Angel, so I ran to help her out. Between us, we got ahold of him and dragged him outside.

Eventually, Pat came out. Her shoulders slumped and the lines between her eyes looked deeper, caked with the heavy makeup. She wasn't the animated star she'd been when the cameras were running. She looked beat. "The producer was there," she said. "He saw it all."

"I'm really sorry, Pat," I said. "I should have kept a closer hold on him." I tried to think of how I could make it up to her. There was no point now in asking her if I could help with the family cooking; her mood was too shot for that discussion. "Maybe I could, um, come on your show and do some Mexican food with you?" The kids had told me that Pat sometimes brought them on her show.

Pat ignored me.

"I mean, you can't cook real Mexican food from cans, but maybe I could give you a fresh touch," I added desperately, knowing even as I said it that she'd take it as a criticism.

"Thanks, Linda, but I think you've done enough."

"Yeah, Linda," Jen chimed in.

Pat glared at her. "I hold you just as responsible. You were told to keep Angel with you."

Jen gave me a dirty look, and I knew I'd lost a friend.

You always wanted to be on a cooking show, a little regretful voice said inside me.

It was a good thing I had myself to talk to, because no one else spoke to me the whole way home.

Fresh from Pittsburgh with Trevor and Leslie

<u>CLICK</u> FOR MORE PICTURES

RELATIONSHIP STATUS:
Married

INTERESTS: Organic food
and gardening, our second
grader, health

What we're cooking: A simple stir-fry with locally grown winter squash and organic turkey

What else we're doing: Recovering from a close encounter with a super-aggressive kid

What we're learning: How kids' behavior is linked to what they eat— <u>check out our Samantha enjoying some healthy Alaskan salmon and brown rice–pumpkin medley</u>—it can be done, parents!

What makes us laugh: Video footage of a kid high on canned food—check it out <u>here</u>

Friends/Family/Foodie Comments:
NYC Cook says: A-D-D City!
Fresh Mom says: That's caused by preservatives. Give the kid some greens!

Chapter Fifteen

Maybe I was trying to get back on Pat's good side the next Sunday—she'd been basically ignoring me since I'd brought Angel to the television studio. I got up and dressed for church without my usual complaints and even got Angel ready, too.

"Come on, *chicolito*, we're going to church," I said in a peppy way, and loud enough so that Pat could hear.

But that had the opposite effect of what I wanted. When Angel realized what day it was and where we were going, he started howling. Too late, I remembered that he did this every week.

"I was hoping to finish my coffee in peace before his Sunday tantrum started up," Pat snapped as she slammed down her cup of instant coffee.

"Sorry. Jeez! I'll take him outside." I picked him up and carried him out into the cold November air. Why couldn't Pat ever notice anything good I did? It was starting to seem more and more likely that she would kick me and Angel out. And no matter how bad it was at Pat's house, foster care would be worse.

Mrs. Piotrowski came out of her house in a dress, and I went over to say hi, Angel trailing along behind me, still crying.

Mrs. Piotrowski pulled some rosary beads out of her coat pocket. "Look. Pretty," she said, dangling them in front of Angel to quiet him down.

The expression that crossed his face was priceless: amazement, excitement, joy, and sadness all rolled into one. *"Mamá,"* he cried, and held out his hands.

I opened my mouth to tell Mrs. P to keep the beads to herself, but she'd already handed them over. I waited for him to rip them apart and for God to shoot a lightning bolt from the sky. But to my surprise, Angel fondled them reverently and started saying an Our Father.

A lightbulb turned on in my head. "Angel," I said, squatting down in front of him, "did your *mamá* have beads like this?"

He nodded.

"Did you go to church with her? To *la iglesia?"*

"Sí, sí."

I looked at Mrs. Piotrowski. "Maybe that's his problem. He's Catholic, and maybe he hates the church we go to."

"I don't know," Mrs. P said doubtfully. "Most kids like that big church your family goes to better, I'm sure. All those bells and whistles."

Even though I'd been raised Catholic, too, I *did* like Pat's church, with its big, airy worship center, modern music, and fun programs for kids. "But maybe he feels bad because of his mom." Suddenly, I saw a chance to make things up to Pat. "Look, can Angel and me come to church with you?"

"Of course, dear. But my daughter's picking me up any minute. And you need to tell Pat."

"That's okay, we're ready." I ran to the door, grabbed Isaiah, and told him to let Pat know where we were.

Angel lived up to his name at mass. He sat looking around

the cathedral, breathing in the incense and staring at the priest like he'd finally come home.

I actually felt the same way, kind of. Back home, Aunt Elba and I had gone to mass most weeks and felt guilty when we didn't. Although the environment and the service were a little different here, it had the same feel. We were a lot more peaceful when we left than when we'd come in. By the time we got home, I was even feeling serene and spiritual about Pat.

Until she completely attacked me! "You can't just go off like that!" she yelled as soon as we walked in the doorway. "You have to learn to ask permission, Linda!"

"It's not like we were going to a bar or something," I said as my good mood seeped away. "We went to mass with Mrs. Piotrowski, and I told Isaiah where we were going."

"Key word *told*. You have got to learn to ask, Linda, especially where Angel is concerned. I had visions of him trashing the altar, for pity's sake."

"Sorry." I even was, a little. "I was trying to make things better. Get him off your shoulders for a couple of hours."

"You're not an only kid anymore. You have to learn to compromise." She heaved a giant sigh. "Okay. Live and learn, I guess." Sir Dad, who'd been standing by not saying anything, opened his arms; and she let him hug her, resting her cheek against his chest. "But I don't know how much more of the learning side I can take," she added.

How could I do anything to fix things when every effort I made with her just botched it up more?

I was still in a bad mood the next day when I met Nick in the school library for math tutoring. That morning Chloe had used my towel and then thrown it on the wet bathroom floor. So I'd yelled at her, and she'd yelled back, and then Pat had yelled at both of us. Not to mention, Jen had barely spoken to me since the incident at the studio.

Pat, Chloe, and Jen—and the risk of being drop-kicked into foster care—weren't the only reasons for my mood. The truth was, I was super homesick. Thanksgiving was coming, and I wondered what Pat would do to celebrate it: pull a turkey out of a can?

Back home, we'd usually gotten together with our restaurant cook, Juan, and his family. We'd spend the whole day cooking a mix of traditional turkey and tasty Tex-Mex. The day was all about food and friends, cooking and togetherness; and it had always been my favorite holiday.

Not this year.

To make a bad day worse, all of my clothes had been dirty in the morning, so I'd swiped one of Chloe's black skirts. It was shorter and tighter than what I usually wore, and when Nick saw me, he looked like someone had brought him cherries jubilee on a platter.

I was too cranky to pretend it wasn't happening. "Stop drooling and teach me some math," I ordered, chucking him on the chin to close his slightly open mouth.

"Yes, ma'am," he said, grinning.

I rolled my eyes and slammed down my books, earning a *"Sssh!"* from the librarian. When I glared at her, who did I see across the room but Dino, staring at me and Nick.

I didn't even grace him with a nod. I was still mad at him for how he'd acted in cooking class the other day.

But I *did* scoot my chair closer to Nick. Let Dino think I had the hots for his cousin. Let him think I didn't give a flip about him.

Once Nick got on task, he was pretty helpful with my homework. The stuff made sense when he explained it slowly, and I realized I'd learned some of it last year; it was just that my books back home had explained everything a little differently, and I hadn't recognized what type of problems they were. After forty-five minutes, I had two days' worth of homework done, and I pretty much understood what we were covering for the rest of the week.

"You want to meet tomorrow?" Nick asked as I stood up. "We could get a jump on next week's work."

I had to laugh at how pathetic he was. Pathetic, but nice at least. "Thanks, Nick," I said, "but I think once a week is plenty. Maybe next Wednesday?"

"It's a date," he said kind of loud, looking over my shoulder.

I turned and saw Dino. "Hey," I said, trying not to sound too friendly.

Nick gave my shoulder a possessive squeeze—where did he get off?—and shot a dirty look at Dino as he headed out of the library.

"Hey," Dino said to me. "Where's your next class?"

"Math wing. Why?"

"I'll walk you there."

"Suit yourself." I started out the door. Let him follow me if he wanted to hang.

But even though I was acting cold, I felt a little thrill inside. He was looking at my legs. He was *definitely* looking at my legs.

We'd beat the morning crowd, so the hallways weren't the usual mob scene. He fell into step beside me. "You like Nick?" he asked.

"He's my math tutor," I said. Of course, that didn't answer his question. If he was jealous, it served him right.

"Do you really have a date with him?"

I shrugged. "My social life is my business." Inside I was giggling and shaking, and I couldn't believe I was actually playing him like this. It wasn't like I had any experience with guys!

"Maybe we could get together sometime," he said. His face

was kind of red, and he sounded out of breath.

I didn't answer because I couldn't. Was he asking me out? Was I even allowed to date here? The subject hadn't come up at home, but I had a strong feeling the answer would be no.

And then from somewhere inside me came the perfect response. "I really don't go out much," I said, and looked sideways to check out his reaction.

None. Well, maybe a little jaw clenching.

"But," I said, and paused until he looked at me. "I *would* like to see your family's restaurant, or deli, or whatever. If you wouldn't mind showing it to me."

Two days later, right after the last bell rang, Dino and I met in the alley behind the school. He was still trying to keep his life as a deli owner's son a secret, and I didn't want Chloe on my case.

It was the day before Thanksgiving break, and I'd picked up everyone's excitement about a few days off from school . . . even though I wouldn't get to be with Aunt Elba, or Juan and his family, or Julia.

"You ready?" Dino growled out of the side of his mouth, pulling his baseball cap down like a gangster.

I giggled and took an exaggerated look around. "Let's roll."

As we walked quickly toward the street behind the school, I saw Chloe and another girl come out through a side door. "Duck!" I said, and nudged Dino behind a Dumpster.

He peeked out. "Sarah Hampton. She's a huge gossip. And they're coming this way."

We edged along the Dumpster to the back and stepped behind it, bumping against each other. Our breaths made steamy clouds in the November air. I was all bundled up in my padded jacket, but Dino wore his leather one open. He held one finger to his lips as he peeked out.

Sarah was telling Chloe about how she'd seen one of the girls from the poetry club making out with a guy from another school. Definitely a gossip, and I was sort of surprised that Chloe was interested. She wasn't the gossipy type.

Of course, if she saw me hanging out with the guy she liked, she'd definitely have something to say.

Chloe stopped right by the Dumpster, raised the lid, and threw something inside.

The odor of rotting food that came out was overpowering, and I couldn't help coughing.

"What was that?" Sarah asked.

I ducked down, gripping Dino's arm so I wouldn't fall over. I really, really didn't want her to find me here with him, hiding from her. That would cement the badness of our relationship, not to mention that she'd probably go running home to Pat to tell on me for betraying her.

"Who knows?" Chloe said. "Probably rats, knowing this school." She banged the Dumpster lid shut, and they continued on.

When it was safe, we crept out. "That was close," Dino said.

"No kidding."

"Come on, we'll go the other way around the block. We've got a bus to catch!"

Running together through the cold streets, looking out to avoid anyone we knew, made me feel like a kid playing. We barely made the bus; and when we got on, we couldn't stop laughing.

I was having so much fun I almost felt guilty. How would Chloe feel if she could see me now?

Dino told me about Pittsburgh landmarks as we rode down to the Strip: Bloomfield, a little shopping district with great old stores and restaurants; the Church Brew House, an actual cathedral that was now a brew pub and restaurant. "My dad hates that place. They actually make beer where the altar used to be."

"Wonder if that's a venial or a mortal sin?"

"You're Catholic!"

"Born and bred." I smiled at him, and a small spark tingled through me.

A bad-smelling bum got on and lurched against me—the bus was getting crowded—so Dino made me move next to the window. When it was time to get off the bus, he kept a hand on my back to guide me through, and yelled for the driver to stop when he started to close the bus doors before we could get off.

It was fun being here with someone who knew his way around.

We walked about a block through the Strip—now much quieter than it had been on Saturday morning—and Dino waved to shopkeepers and the few brave street vendors who were out. I liked how he was in his element. I liked him a *lot*.

When we walked through the doorway of Moretti's Italian Market and Deli, I was practically assaulted, but in a good way. First were the smells: bread baking, garlicky sauces, spicy pepperoni. Plus the sounds: people talking loudly in Italian and English, pots banging, a radio playing. And then there was Dino's father, who'd yelled at Dino the last time I was down here, coming toward us with a big wooden spoon in his hand.

Instinctively I cringed, and he noticed. He cuffed Dino on the side of his head, lightly, and then put an arm around me. "What, you're afraid of me? What lies has this one told you?"

"It's not that," I said. "My aunt used to whack me with a wooden spoon when I was in trouble. She's a cook, too."

"Ah, cooking in the family. That's a good thing. Come along. My son will show you around."

Someone called from the back, where most of the cooking sounds and smells came from, and Dino's dad hurried off.

"My dad's crazy," Dino said apologetically. "So what do you want to see?"

"Everything," I said.

"Be my guest."

I wandered up and down the aisles of the market with Dino closer than he needed to be behind me. My heart hammered a lot faster than necessary as I walked past the bins of olives, the deli counter brimming with meats and cheeses, and the various types of pasta. When I got to a section of canned goods imported from Italy, I started cracking up. "I should get some of this stuff for Pat," I said.

"You think she'd go for it?"

"It's canned." I was actually tempted. She probably would. "But I'd have to tell Chloe I came down here, and . . ."

"What? It's okay. You already spilled my secret to Chloe."

"Yeah, but she . . ." I trailed off. As mad as I got at Chloe sometimes, I couldn't rat her out on the fact that she liked Dino. And thinking about Chloe made me feel sneaky and bad for enjoying Dino's company. "She's weird. I'd better not." *And I'd better change the subject, fast.* "Does your mom work down here, too?"

Dino shook his head and got very busy straightening up some boxes of rice that were slightly, but not really, out of order. Okay, I could read that he didn't want to talk about his mom. That made me curious, but I let it go.

Now what? We'd walked through the whole market, and we were out of conversation. Would he think I was a boring idiot because I wasn't as lively and talky as girls like Mindy and Mandy?

"Want to see our kitchen?" Dino offered. "We could probably score some fresh bread."

"Definitely."

Everyone in the kitchen joked with Dino, and his dad made him mix up a batch of antipasto dressing. The whole thing felt more like home than anyplace I'd been in Pittsburgh so far. This was where I wanted to be. This was so much better than Pat's home kitchen with canned everything. And it even outshone the pristine kitchen of Pat's cooking show.

Dino was a different person here than he was at school: relaxed and fun. Why on earth did he want to be the shallow popular kid instead of the far cooler real person he was down here?

When he got done with his jobs and came over to where I was perched on a stool just soaking everything in, I asked him.

He shrugged. "I don't know." But I could tell that he was hiding something.

"I'm serious." I frowned at him. "This is the coolest place. Lots of kids at school would think so. Why don't you show it off?"

His father heard that and shook his head. "He's ashamed of the way we live. Ashamed of the business that puts a fine leather jacket on his back." Again he cuffed Dino's head, which I was beginning to recognize as a gesture of affection.

Dino ducked away. "When I was little, kids teased me about smelling like garlic," he said. "Called me names. What can I say? It traumatized me."

He was joking, but not.

"Oh, my gosh, so when I said you smelled good—"

"Yep, bad memories."

"I'm sorry," I said. "I just . . ." I wanted to say something, but I felt shy suddenly.

"What?"

I shook my head. "I'd better go. I have to catch the bus home."

"I'm walking you to the bus stop."

So I said good-bye to everyone, and got a pat on the shoulder from his dad and an invitation to come back anytime. Dino and I walked out into the cold wind.

"You're not off the hook," he said as we wrapped our coats closer around us, shivering. "You were going to say something back there."

I looked at him. He had really nice brown eyes. And they were looking steadily, but teasingly, at me.

"I was going to say," I said slowly, "that you *do* smell good."

He wrapped an arm around me and pulled me to his side. Pushing back a strand of my hair, he whispered into my ear, "So do you."

His breath felt warm on the side of my face, and his body warm beside me; and I was suddenly feeling things I didn't know how to handle.

Thank Our Lady—or *not*—for the bus that came lumbering down the street toward us.

Linda Delgado

CLICK FOR MORE PICTURES

RELATIONSHIP STATUS:
Single

INTERESTS: Food, friends, more food, fun!

What I'm cooking today:
Italian Antipasto: Recipe for Love!!!

Ingredients:
1 cup olive oil
½ cup wine vinegar (part balsamic if desired)
Fresh garlic, oregano, and basil to taste
Salt & pepper

Mix all ingredients and toss with:
Chopped cauliflower, carrots, and peppers
Pepperoni
Olives
Cannelloni beans

Refrigerate at least one hour. Enjoy with someone who loves food and praises your cooking, and see what happens next!

Friends/Family/Foodie Comments:
Julia says: Linda! What aren't you telling me?!

Ima Foodie says: You've got to be kidding. Oily, garlicky antipasto is delicious, but hardly romantic.

Italian Stallion says: Loosen up, Ima. Obviously you're not Italian. Linda, what's your phone number?

FABFOODZ.COM

HOME | PROFILE | FRIENDS | RECIPES

Julia Payette

<u>CLICK</u> FOR MORE PICTURES

RELATIONSHIP STATUS:
Single

INTERESTS: Reading, computers, cooking. (Yeah, I'm a geek.)

What I'm cooking today:
Easy Navajo Peach Pudding

Ingredients:
Instant pudding—vanilla
3–4 fresh peaches
Honey and pine nuts to taste

• Peel all but one peach and puree the peeled peaches in blender.
• Mix up the pudding according to package directions.
• Add peach puree to pudding.

• Chop the remaining peach, and sprinkle it over the pudding along with some honey and pine nuts.

Friends/Family/Foodie Comments:
Linda says: Sounds yummy!
Julia says: OMG, I can't believe you said something nice about a recipe with instant pudding in it!
Linda says: Am I that much of a food snob?
Misty says: I'll help you make some!

Chapter Sixteen

The next day was Thanksgiving. I woke up feeling giddy and nervous about Dino. Did he *like* like me? Did I like him that way? And what did that mean? I had no idea how to go about having a boyfriend.

When I looked over at Chloe, still snoring lightly in her bed, my excitement turned to guilt. This was going to upset her if it happened.

But maybe it wasn't really happening at all. I knew from watching boys and girls flirt that it could all be a bunch of nothing.

I was so confused that I followed my nose into the kitchen. Was that turkey I smelled, or was I hallucinating?

It was! And no one was around, which was good, because I was itching to deal with my mixed-up feelings through cooking. Pat wouldn't like it; but after all, it was Thanksgiving, and I wanted to express my thankfulness just like anybody else. I wasn't going to try to cook a whole dinner, but we could use some fresh rolls to go with the canned stuff.

I rummaged around until I found flour, water, and butter. There was some antique-looking yeast, too; I didn't trust it, so I threw on my winter coat over my jammies and ran next door.

Sure enough, Mrs. Piotrowski was up and glad to give me some yeast from her well-stocked cupboard. I even invited her to come over for Thanksgiving dinner later, but she was planning to have dinner with her daughters out in the suburbs. "If you need anything else, just come on back," she said.

People were starting to stir at home, so I hurried up and got the dough for the rolls going. Working with my hands, testing the warm water, and watching the yeast bubble helped me calm down.

By the time Pat rolled in, looking pale and sleepy, I couldn't be stopped.

She looked at my flour-covered apron suspiciously. "What have you been up to?"

"Just making rolls for Thanksgiving dinner, that's all," I said, and put an arm around her. "Happy Thanksgiving. Want some coffee or a bowl of cereal?"

Amazingly, she didn't order me to stop cooking. Instead, she sat down heavily. "Coffee, please," she said. "I was planning to make canned biscuits. I'm feeling too sick to deal with anything complicated."

"All the more reason to let other people help," I said, putting the dishes I'd been using into the sink to wash. "Besides, no one cooks Thanksgiving dinner by themselves. *Especially* somebody with this many kids."

"We agreed to a moratorium on discussing this," she said.

"We didn't agree to it; you ordered it. And anyway, I'm not discussing your cooking. I'm just cooking."

Out in the living room, somebody turned on the TV to the Macy's Thanksgiving Day Parade. Upstairs, I heard a shower go on. Everyone was waking up.

A few minutes later, Jen bounced into the kitchen. She was still in her pajamas—red-and-white striped leggings and a long white T-shirt—but she looked perky and wide-awake. "Everybody ready for my famous green bean casserole?" she asked. "If I start it cooking now, it'll be ready in time."

Neither Pat nor I answered, but that didn't stop Jen. She disappeared into the pantry and started pulling out industrial-sized cans.

Pat and I looked at each other. I could read what she was thinking from her guilty expression. She let Jen cook, so why not me?

Of course, the difference was in the contents. I would never fall into line with *Cooking from Cans* the way that Jen did.

For example, right now, *what* was Jen bringing out? Ugh. Canned green beans, canned mushroom soup, and . . . what was that, canned fried onions? Was there a vitamin in the entire recipe?

I opened my mouth to comment and then shut it again. Jen just looked so happy.

Sir Dad stuck his head into the kitchen and gave Jen a thumbs-up as she bustled by carrying yet another can. "Green bean casserole?" he asked. "My favorite."

My eyebrows went up, but my mouth stayed shut. No telling what people will like. And holidays are for traditions, not vitamins. It was time for me to start accepting this family for who they were.

Jen peeked into the oven. "Turkey looks huge!" she said. "When did you guys put it in?"

"I was up at five," Pat said.

Whew. No wonder she looked so tired.

Pat put her hands flat on the table and kind of pushed herself out of her seat. "Let's see. I better make the stuffing."

She got out a giant black-and-white box that said STUFFING.

Talk about generic! But I knew better than to argue. I asked if I could make the sweet potatoes, and she looked wary but said yes.

Chloe showed up in the doorway then. Jeez, even her holiday pajamas were black. "What are you guys doing?" she asked, rubbing her eyes.

"Cooking," Jen and I chorused.

Chloe raised her eyebrows and looked at her mom, who was stirring stuffing in a giant bowl. Then she padded over to the refrigerator and pulled out a cola. If that was her breakfast, it was no surprise why she was crabby all the time.

"Do you want some cereal or toast or something?" I asked her.

She blinked at me. "Huh?"

"Breakfast? Hello? I'll make you some?"

"Good lord, what's gotten into you?" she asked. But she accepted the bowl of cereal I poured for her.

I looked in the oven at the turkey. "Pat. Do you want me to baste that?"

She glanced over her shoulder. "It'll be fine."

"Really? It could get dry."

"I've got it covered." Her voice was a little tight.

"Actually, it's *not* covered," I said. "Now if you put a foil tent over it—"

"Your turkey usually *is* just a teeny bit dry, Mom," Jen cut in. I was happy to know she had my back again.

"Yeah, like the Sahara desert," Chloe added.

Pat spun around to scold us, then put one hand to her stomach and the other on a chair back. She looked . . . wobbly. "I give up. You girls finish the dinner. I'm going back to bed."

Linda Delgado

<u>CLICK</u> FOR MORE PICTURES

RELATIONSHIP STATUS:
Single

INTERESTS: Food, friends, more food, fun!

What I'm cooking today:
Thanksgiving dinner! Check out my <u>recipe</u> for yeast rolls.

What else I'm doing: Nothing—this is a full-time job!

Friends/Family/Foodie Comments:
Julia says: Happy TG, babe. Is Pat making canned turkey or something?
Linda says: No, it's real. But I've got to get a foil tent on it, like, now.
Ima Foodie says: Hey, I'm putting this together. Is your mom Pat from Cooking from Cans?
Linda says: No comment.
Hank says: OMG, the famous Pat! Tell us about her TG dinner.
Linda says: Can't! Too much to do. But check out her recipe for <u>green bean casserole</u>—I just posted it.

Chapter Seventeen

Jen and Chloe stared as Pat walked out of the kitchen. "Great day to go on strike, Mom," Chloe called, but Pat didn't turn around.

"That's not like Mom," Jen said, wrinkling her nose. "She's been acting weird lately."

"Well, she is getting *older*," Chloe said. "Don't women get kind of . . . cranky or something in middle age?"

"Some of them don't wait that long." I looked at Chloe and then ducked when she tossed a pot holder at me.

"The real question is, do either of you have a clue about how to cook a turkey?" Jen asked. "Because I don't. And no way are Sir Dad and the boys going to be any help."

"I do," I said. "Where's the foil?"

Jen and Chloe fell right into line, following my orders. Within ten minutes we had a foil tent over the newly basted turkey. After another quick visit to Mrs. Piotrowski's house, we had fresh celery and onions to liven up that generic stuffing. I put Chloe to work peeling white potatoes—even Pat didn't buy those canned—and got Jen busy on a cranberry relish plate. I chopped some pecans I'd found in the back of the cupboard as a topping for the sweet potatoes. When the twins, Hector and Veta, came in hunting for food, we gave them tortilla chips and made them set the table.

Outside, the sky was gray, and streaks of rain made lines down the windows. Inside, the bubble and scent of butter, sautéing onions, and roasting turkey made the house smell like a party.

"So, what's everyone doing for First Formal?" Jen asked. "I remember how much fun it was my freshman year. I went with Timmy Norton—I thought I was so in love with him— and then he ditched me to talk to his friends from Automotive Repair, so I hooked up with Jeremy Sayers. . . ."

"Jen has war stories," Chloe said to me. "She remembers ninth grade like it was yesterday."

"I do," Jen said, grinning. She had the ability to ignore Chloe's sarcastic side, an amazing feat since Chloe's sarcastic side was pretty much her only side. "So, did either of you get asked yet? It's next week, right?"

"I didn't," I said, focusing on the chopping so my face wouldn't reveal my thoughts. "But I didn't really expect to. Hardly anyone knows me." Inside, I had one huge word in my brain: *Dino*. Was there a chance he'd ask me?

"What about you, Chloe?" Jen asked.

"So you're not going with Dino then?" Chloe said to me.

What did she know? "He didn't ask me." Then I risked honesty. "Though I wouldn't mind. I like him."

Chloe sighed. "Yeah, me, too. But he doesn't know I'm alive." Her voice was glum.

"You both like the same boy?" Jen asked. "That's so cute! I remember when my best friend, Sara, and I liked the same boy. We made a deal: we both went after him; and whoever he chose, the other girl couldn't be mad about it. That way we could have fun planning our campaign together!" She giggled. "We even went out on dates, all three of us."

"Who won?" I asked.

Chloe rolled her eyes. "Who do you think?"

"I did," Jen said modestly. "But to tell you the truth, by the time he asked me out I liked someone else, so Sara ended up dating him."

I had to laugh. Jen was so flaky. But I liked her positive attitude about life. "We're all on the refreshment committee," I told her, "me, Chloe, and Dino. So maybe we'll all end up desperate and dateless at the dance."

"You're all three on the committee?" she asked, her eyes widening.

"We *are* the committee." Chloe's voice was disgusted. "Just us three. Nice and cozy."

"But that's perfect!" Jen said.

Sir Dad poked his head into the kitchen. "You girls need any help?"

"It's under control," I said.

"Daddy." Jen pulled him into the kitchen. "We need the man's point of view. Both Chloe and Linda like the same boy, and they're all on the refreshment committee for the freshman dance. Shouldn't they both dress up and pick him up and take him?"

"Like a double date, only with just one boy?" Sir Dad said, chuckling. "It'll be *his* dream come true."

"But then he can choose, right?" Jen was practically jumping up and down. "And whoever's left over will be at the dance with lots of other people, so she's sure to have a good time."

"You mean *you'd* have a good time in that situation," Chloe said. "I doubt I would."

"And I don't have a dress," I said. "I was planning to wear

casual clothes and stay behind the scenes."

Jen waved a hand. "I have the perfect dress for you to borrow. It's red. It'll look great with your dark coloring. Don't you think so, Dad?"

Sir Dad lifted his hands and backed out of the kitchen. "I'm not the person to ask about fashion," he said. "Let me know if you need any help with dinner."

My yeast dough had risen, so I rolled it out and showed Jen and Chloe how to cut triangles and fold them over with a pat of butter inside each. Yum!

"I'm so glad you're here, Linda," Jen gushed. "What would we do without you to help us cook?"

I was actually having a surprisingly good time, but I also missed Aunt Elba, Juan and his family, and the yummy spicy food we'd all cooked together. "I miss being with people I've known my whole life," I admitted, "but I'm grateful to this family for taking me in. I guess that's what I'm thankful for today."

"Yeah, that's one thing this family is good at: taking people in," Chloe muttered.

"And you hate it," Jen accused.

"Yeah, sometimes. People at school tease me about being in this family. Especially when certain people"—she looked at me—"spill the beans about how many kids we have."

"Sorry." The funny thing was, I'd started to see what made Chloe so sensitive. People *did* stare at our family when everyone showed up together somewhere, even church. It wasn't just the big number of kids, but the fact that everyone was a different color.

"What's wrong with having a lot of kids?" Jen asked. "I think it's fun. You never have to be alone."

Chloe and I looked at each other. Jen might like never being alone, but I felt differently, and I knew Chloe did, too.

"Anyway," Jen said, "if you act like it's something you're

ashamed of, kids will tease you. But if you act like you love it and are thrilled about it, they'll leave you alone."

I stared at Jen. "Is your peppy stuff an act?"

She grinned. "Not completely. I'm a pretty happy person. But I do always play up the positive side, and it works to keep people off my case. Believe it or not, I could be as gloomy as Chloe if I thought about all the bad things in my life."

Chloe nodded. "It's the truth. She had a rough time as a little kid."

By this point we were sitting at the table talking. But suddenly there was a loud clatter that scared all of us. We turned to see Angel up on the counter, looking cute—but guilty. The cupboard door was open in front of him, and he held a box of vanilla wafers.

"What did you do?" I asked.

"Lo siento," he said, gesturing toward the green bean casserole cooling on the counter.

We all rushed over. Sitting in the casserole was a salt canister, open, its contents spilling into the beans.

"You ruined it, you little devil," Jen said, yanking him off the counter and dropping him to the floor.

"Hey! No child abuse," Chloe said.

Angel started wailing.

I squatted down, hugging Angel and wiping his tears. "She hurt me; she's mean!" he yelled, pointing at Jen. *"¡No está permitido!"*

"Just take the salt canister out and scoop away the salty part," I told her. "No one'll know the difference." *It's already got enough sodium to give us the family world record for high blood pressure.*

"He's always messing things up for me," Jen complained as she tried to follow my directions. "I can't wait until . . ." She trailed off, but in my mind I finished her sentence. *Until he's gone.*

Angel must have done the same thing, because he stiffened

in my arms, then started bawling louder.

"How do you think that makes him feel?" I glared at Jen. For someone so positive, she could be pretty mean when it came to Angel. "He knows perfectly well what you were about to say."

"Come on, kiddo, let's clean you up," Chloe said, suddenly swooping in.

My surprise must have shown on my face.

Chloe shrugged. "You've got to get dinner on the table, right?"

"Yeah. Thanks." I handed Angel over. Then I got the turkey out, tested the drumstick, and determined that it was done. It looked golden brown and smelled wonderful. We popped the rolls into the oven. Sir Dad filled water glasses while Jen woke up Pat and called everyone to come down.

I surveyed the meal and smiled. I hadn't had much to work with, but it was going to be a decent Thanksgiving dinner. And I felt as if I'd played an important role in pulling it together. They couldn't have done it without me, and that felt good.

We loaded up the table, and everyone joined hands for a prayer. As we stood, holding hands around the table, I got a fuzzy feeling in my heart, half sad and half happy. I missed Aunt Elba, but I was enjoying this, too.

Everyone sat down except Sir Dad, who was carving, and Jen, who was carrying around her green bean casserole because the dish was too hot to pass. And because she wanted everyone to eat from the nonsalty side of it.

Mashed potatoes, sweet potatoes with a nut topping, rolls, cranberry relish—it all went around the table. Comments like "You're a goddess, Linda," and "Cook for us every day, please" didn't hurt my ego one bit. I just hoped everyone's nice reactions didn't upset Pat.

"Linda, I hope you stay with us forever," Isaiah said.

"I don't care about staying here." Angel shot a defiant look around the table. "I. Don't. Care."

Sudden silence.

My heart twisted as I tried to think of something reassuring to say. But I couldn't, and I looked at Pat for help.

"Let's think positive," Pat said. "We're all together for now, and we can be thankful for that."

Angel stared at his plate, then grabbed three rolls from the basket and started shoving them into his mouth.

I happened to look at Jen. She was watching him, a stricken expression on her face.

"Turkey's moist this year," Sir Dad said in a hearty voice, obviously trying to get the conversation back on track.

Chloe, Pat, Jen, and I exchanged glances.

"Must have been the tent," Jen said.

"It was a really good turkey," I said, trying to give Pat some credit.

Pat opened her mouth, and I thought she was going to complain about the changes we'd made to her dinner plan. Instead, she took a deep breath and put down the dish she was holding.

"I'm not feeling too well," she said. "I'm kind of dizzy."

Then, as if in slow motion, she slumped sideways until she was lying curled up on the bench seat, passed out.

Chapter Eighteen

For me it was déjà vu. Just a couple of months ago, Aunt Elba had gotten sick and had to be rushed to the hospital. Now it was Pat. Even though she woke up a few minutes later and insisted she was fine, Sir Dad drove her to the emergency room right away.

She didn't stay in the hospital long, though. The doctors figured out her problem pretty quickly: she was pregnant! *That* was what her tiredness and sickness and crabbiness was all about.

The whole family flipped out over the news. Sir Dad was ecstatic; they'd wanted to have more kids after Chloe but couldn't, and that was why they'd adopted so many.

"I can't believe she's pregnant," Chloe whined after hanging up from a phone call with Sir Dad. It was easy to see why she was upset: she'd had some kind of special status as the only biological child, and that was about to end.

Angel ran around and around the room. "Babies suck," he kept yelling, which I actually thought was funny.

"Angel!" Jen scolded. "Go outside. You're driving me crazy."

Angel ran out, leaving the front door open to let in the freezing November wind. Chloe got up, cursing under her breath, and slammed the door. "It's not like we have enough money for the kids we already have," she groused.

And there was the real problem. Now that they were going to have a baby, would they kick out Angel and me?

I went out on the porch, thinking I'd play with Angel a little; but the cold wind and gloomy sky sent me back inside.

So I called Aunt Elba. I wanted her to sympathize, but she sounded as crabby as the rest of us. "My mother is driving me crazy in the kitchen," she said after I'd called her out for snapping at me. "Linda, you'll just have to cope with the situation until I speak with Pat. I'm way too tired right now."

Jen was on the homework computer while I was talking to Aunt Elba, and as soon as I clicked off my phone, she attacked. "Do you know why I love that casserole?" she demanded.

"What're you talking about?"

"That recipe you posted on your FabFoodz page. The one everyone's mocking now."

"You saw my page?"

"Mostly I look at Mom's. And you'd better count your blessings that she's technology shy. People are figuring out your connection to her."

I shrugged. "Do that many people really care about a kid's page?"

"Yeah, they do. And now they're making fun of a recipe that means the world to me."

I coughed into my hand to hide my giggle. "Jen, why does green bean casserole mean so much to you?" I kept waiting for Jen's usual good humor—heck, her *sense* of humor—to resurface.

But it wasn't happening. Instead, Jen yanked me into the empty kitchen and shoved me into a chair. Then she sat down across the table from me. "You know how you read about abused and neglected kids who go through the garbage to find food?"

"Yeah, I guess," I said, though I'd never heard of anything like that.

"Well, I was one of those kids. Up to the time I was five, I lived with my drug addict mom, when she was around; and most of the time she didn't feed me. Did you ever wonder why I'm so petite?"

I shrugged. "I thought you liked it that way."

Jen shrugged. "I make the best of it; but the truth is, my growth was stunted because of malnutrition."

My stomach lurched as I stared at her. "That's . . . really awful, Jen." And I meant it.

She nodded. "When Pat finally adopted me, she did feed me. And feed me, and feed me."

"Wow. I didn't know."

"Green bean casserole was the first vegetable I ever ate, and the only one I liked. She made it for me every night for months."

"Oh." I didn't know what to say.

"So have a little compassion, okay? There are people who need comfort food. And who are you, Miss Always Had Plenty To Eat, to judge them?"

I lifted my hands, palms out. "Sorry."

"No, you're not; but you should be."

As she stomped out of the room, I remembered the recipes Aunt Elba had from her grandmother, the ones with the hearts and flowers drawn all over them. And then I thought about the recipes from her mean mother.

Which kind of cook did I want to be, anyway? A loving one or a cruel one? "I really am sorry, Jen," I called after her in a lame way.

With everyone in such a crazy mood, it was a relief to get back to school that Monday. Miss Xavier was thrilled with the plan I had decided on: to cook empanadas for the dance. And the girls in cooking class were happy about the low-calorie benefits of cut-up fruit.

And when Dino came up to me at my locker after English and asked me to go to a poetry slam that night, I got superexcited. This was a real date, my first!

Okay, it would get us extra credit in English, so it was just a homework-type date. But then again, we'd get to sit in the audience together and hear our fellow students reading their poetry. I imagined low lights and soft, tender words. It could turn out to be really romantic.

When we got there, though, my romantic dreams crashed and burned. That was because—surprise, surprise—Chloe was on the program. And when she saw me walk in with Dino, she got furious.

She cornered me in the bathroom. "What do you think you're doing?"

"Um, coming to a poetry reading?" I breathed in stuffy air scented with chemical cleaners and tried to go on the offensive. "I thought you'd be glad I'm supporting you."

"Dad's here, and that's all the support I need," she said. "I *don't* need to look out in the audience and see you trying to steal my boyfriend!"

"Your boyfriend?" I huffed. "Have you ever even gone out with him?"

"No." Chloe's eyes got watery, threatening to ruin her heavy black makeup. "No, it's true; he's never asked me to do anything. But that doesn't matter to me. I'm in love with him, Linda, and it almost killed me to see you walk in with him. We're family. You're not supposed to do this to me!"

A couple of girls from our school came into the bathroom

then, so Chloe didn't say any more. Instead, she stalked out.

Her words totally spoiled my fun. Usually Chloe was so extreme and weird that I could laugh her off. But just now she'd sounded sincere and almost normal in her admission of love. And if she *loved* Dino . . . well, who was I to interfere with that? I liked him, but love wasn't something I knew anything about.

Dino was browsing the magazines when I came out, and he beckoned me over. "Check this out," he said, and showed me one of those crazy "Chimp Abducted by Aliens"–type newspapers. I laughed; but when he let his hand rest on my shoulder, I couldn't help glancing back to see whether Chloe noticed.

She was watching us, her face twisted like she was about to cry.

I moved away from Dino, feeling kind of resentful at the same time. Why did I have to be the one to give him up? Having a boy like Dino interested in me was practically the best thing in my world right now. Chloe was in her own home, with her own family, and had no real problems.

Except that she's just found out her mom's pregnant, my conscience reminded me.

And remember, she's your cousin.

Dino cleared his throat and moved closer. "Hey, before the reading starts," he said, "I wanted to tell you I thought about what you said at our market. I do have more fun when I'm being myself."

I smiled, pleased that he'd taken my words so seriously. "Seems like you do."

"Anyway, thanks." He gave me a little squeeze around the shoulders.

I immediately tensed. Was Chloe watching?

But when I looked up, the glare I caught came from Sir Dad. He looked from Chloe to me and back again. As the facilitator got everything ready for the reading to start, he went up to

Chloe and talked intensely to her. It was like he was her coach and she was a wrestling champ; by the time he finished, she was nodding and looking fierce and determined.

I felt relieved. Even though Chloe bugged me, I didn't want her to screw up at the reading.

The facilitator introduced the participants and then said some kind words about each one's work. A few seconds later Chloe came to the stage.

She cleared her throat, tossed back her jet-black hair, and surveyed the audience. When she held up her pages of poetry, her hands shook so hard that the pages rattled.

"Aw, she's nervous," a woman said, too loud.

"Yeah, and with all those pages, we're in for it," whispered her male friend.

I glared at the couple who'd spoken. I felt as nervous as Chloe. In a strange way, it was as if it was me up there.

"My first poem is called 'O, Romeo,'" she announced, not looking around.

"*Oh, no,*" a kid in front of me whispered.

I held my breath. Would she have that horrible shaky voice I sometimes got when I was nervous? Would she stutter? Would she have to stop before the end and sit down, the way I'd done during my fifth-grade oral report?

But her voice came out steady and strong as she said a few words about composing the poem. I breathed a sigh of relief. Now I could relax and listen.

O, Romeo

"O, happy dagger!"
So cried Juliet.

Smooth and sharp,

but shall soon be stained
by my dark blood.
Bring me out of my despair
by death.
So it seems I will leave this world
by a dagger's kiss.

Juliet
was an idiot.

When the sun came up and then went down,
I bared my heart,
saw the flame of death and mourning.
This is how it ends and starts.
Thousands lost and yet I found
something I'd left behind.
A feeling clean, pure, and true,
but if only I could rewind . . .

Reverse the flow,
go to that moment
and have it with us then
maybe it would all go away . . .

But I remember as I shed my tears
for those who left without good-byes
and as I gaze at that happy dagger,

I am no Juliet.

She cocked her head and smiled, and everyone applauded enthusiastically. Me, too. I'd been ready for dark teen angst, and it was definitely there. But I hadn't counted on Chloe's wicked humor to ease the tension of her more negative concepts. She had everyone laughing with her delivery of the "Juliet" lines, and that meant that we were all with her when she took us to a darker place.

By the time she finished reading two more poems, people nodded and clapped and smiled, and I heard a couple of them saying "Bravo!"

My heart swelled with pride. "That's my cousin," I called out, clapping hard.

I'd almost forgotten Dino was next to me until he tapped me on the arm. "She's really good," he said.

I nodded, smiling.

"It's like I *get* Chloe now," he said thoughtfully as the applause died down and the next person headed to the podium. "I never really understood all that girl-in-black stuff, but now I think I do."

That gave me a twinge. I wanted everyone to like Chloe and appreciate her work, but I didn't know if I wanted Dino to admire her quite that much.

No one else was anywhere near as good, and after the reading, me and Dino and Sir Dad went to congratulate Chloe. We weren't the first; we had to wait in line to talk to her, and when we reached her she was glowing with excitement and pride.

"You did well, daughter," Sir Dad said. That was all he said, but his eyes shone and he pulled her against him in a sidearm hug, and Chloe glowed some more.

"Hey, good stuff," Dino said. "I, um, have to admit I don't like poetry that much, but I liked yours."

Chloe smiled and blushed and was totally tongue-tied. Dino waited for a minute, but when she didn't say anything, he kind of shrugged and turned away.

I mouthed "Talk to him," but Chloe shrugged, her hands lifting helplessly.

Suddenly I knew just what to do. I put my hand on his arm. "Wait," I said. "Dino. Chloe and I are getting her sister, Jen"—I looked at Chloe significantly, hoping she'd understand what I was doing—"to drive us to First Formal. Want to ride along?"

Chloe's eyes widened, and her face got blotchy. I could hear her swallowing hard. It was like she was having a seizure, and not a joyous one. She looked ready to kill me.

"Um, well, you mean we'd all go without dates?" Dino asked.

"Uh-huh." I held my breath. Would he agree?

"Well, I guess I could go with you guys," Dino said doubtfully.

"Linda." Chloe was shooting eight different mad messages to me with her black-rimmed eyes.

"Great," I said. "We'll pick you up at seven with refreshments in hand. Don't forget to dress up."

Linda Delgado

CLICK FOR MORE PICTURES

RELATIONSHIP STATUS:
Single

INTERESTS: Food, friends, more food, fun!

What I'm cooking today:
Empanadas for First Formal

What else I'm doing: Getting ready for my first dance!

Empanadas

• Start with a simple dough of flour, moistened with some egg, shortening, water, and a splash of vinegar.

• Roll it out and cut into circles (harder than it looks!).

• Put filling of your choice in the middle and fold over. We used ground beef, peppers, olives, and raisins (yes, you read that right!). Crimp edges with a fork.

• Brush with butter and egg white, and bake at 350° until done.

Friends/Family/Foodie Comments:

Jenster says: Just you wait—those empanadas can't hold a candle to pigs in blankets.

Linda says: Jen, is that you?

Hank says: What school? Can I meet you?

Julia says: Sounds like high drama!

Misty says: Have fun, Linda! Julia said your empanadas rock!

Jenster says: Everyone, come on over to Pat's Cooking from Cans page tomorrow. You'll see whether the kids preferred foodie food or canned food.

Chapter Nineteen

"It's bad enough that I have to be in a sick love triangle with you," Chloe huffed as we hauled bags of groceries into the house the morning of the dance. "Now I have to cook with you, too?"

"I told you, I'm trying to help by getting you and Dino together at the dance. Besides, you're the one who horned in on the refreshment committee. Dino and I could have done just fine by ourselves."

"Yeah, well, where is Mr. Too Good to Get My Hands Dirty, anyway?"

That was a good question. Even though he was on the refreshment committee for the dance, Dino had made excuse after excuse about helping with the cooking. I didn't see why, when Chloe knew his "shameful" secret about being the son of a deli owner. At least he had promised to bring the cut-up fruit.

We were going to spend the rest of the day making Aunt Elba's empanadas, a major challenge. Chloe wasn't exactly skilled in the kitchen, not to mention her bad attitude, so I could have used Dino's help.

We were lucky that the rest of the kids were out of the way, off cheering on Isaiah and Sam, who'd both made the junior math decathlon.

"Anyway," Chloe whined, "I don't see why we have to go to all this trouble. It's a Cheetos crowd."

"They've just never been introduced to good food," I said. "Kind of like this family. Remember Thanksgiving dinner?"

Jen stood watching us, arms crossed over her chest. "Chloe's right," she said. "School dances aren't about the food. They're about spending the whole day making yourself beautiful."

Chloe and I glanced at each other and rolled our eyes in unison, for once on the same wavelength. Jen was effortlessly beautiful, yet she'd still spend the whole day improving herself. It figured.

Maybe we were making a mistake by focusing on food; but, on the other hand, with our raw material, more time to primp wouldn't necessarily make much difference. "I can get ready in an hour," I said, "as long as someone can give me something for this zit." I'd woken up with a whopper on my chin.

"I guess you can have some of my concealer, but you should put some Dry-Up on it now. It's in the medicine cabinet." Chloe had an arsenal of acne weapons, since her skin tended to break out.

"You two have fun." Jen pushed away from the counter. "I'm going out for a couple of hours, but I'll be back by six to help you get ready. I can't wait."

"Yeah, you and me both," Chloe said with a heavy dose of sarcasm.

I was glad Jen seemed to have forgiven me for posting her recipe.

An hour and a half later, Chloe and I were covered with sticky puff pastry dough and flour, and we only had half as much as we needed rolled out.

Chloe swiped the rolling pin viciously over the dough. "Aaaah! It broke again. Linda, just say it: this is a disaster."

"It wouldn't be if you would try harder." But I wasn't so sure. Making puff pastry with Aunt Elba had been fun; but she'd always known how to keep the dough to the exact right temperature, how much flour to add, and when to take a break. Now that I was in charge, I had to admit that I wasn't doing very well.

"I hate this," Chloe grouched. "We'll never get done in time for the dance."

Chloe's loud, upset voice brought Sir Dad into the room. "Have you backward planned?" he asked. "What's your ETD?"

"Huh?" I asked.

"Estimated time of departure, and we're getting close." Chloe dropped her head onto her elbows right on top of the dough, creating two more holes in it.

"Watch it!" I lifted her from behind and moved her to a clear spot. "We have four hours." I checked the kitchen clock, and my stomach tightened. "Or actually, three."

"Let's just get some frozen pizza rolls. No one will ever know," Chloe said.

I was almost tempted, but my pride wouldn't let me cave in.

"Isn't there a third member of this committee?" Sir Dad asked. "Why don't you call him?" He looked around. "He could at least help you clean up this kitchen before your mother gets home from the hospital." Pat was back in for more tests related to her pregnancy, an all-day proposition, which was why we even had access to the forbidden kitchen.

"Okay, we'll call Dino," Chloe said. "And we'll ask him about the frozen pizza rolls idea. I know he'll be on my side."

After listening to her whine into the phone about the disastrous puff pastry, I expected Dino to side with her. Instead she listened, getting even frownier.

Finally she turned and thrust the phone at me. "He says we

won't get our grade if we go fake," she snarled, "and he wants to talk to you."

"Look," he said as soon as I greeted him, "you can get frozen puff pastry at Giant Eagle. Why are you killing yourself for homemade?"

I heard myself snort. "You can't freeze puff pastry."

"Miracles of modern technology. My dad uses it all the time."

"But—"

"Linda," he said, "the filling will still be homemade. And Chloe says you guys aren't even halfway finished. You have to compromise."

Grr, that word.

"Well . . ." I hesitated.

"Just do it." He paused, then added, "But don't tell anyone it was my idea."

"You could help by—"

"Gotta go," he said.

Ooh, I was so ready to kill him. Mr. Romantic at the poetry reading was Mr. Useless when there was work to be done.

But I had to admit that his suggestion about the frozen pastry was a good one.

Sir Dad offered to take Chloe to get the frozen pastry while I cleaned up the kitchen and started on the filling. I gave a mild protest against doing all that work myself, but I'd sort of asked for it, as Chloe oh so snarkily pointed out.

As soon as they'd pulled out of the driveway, I called Aunt Elba. Her voice age-regressed me enough years that I started to cry like a six-year-old.

"*Cara, cara,*" she soothed me, and made me tell her all about what was going on. She was thrilled to hear that we were cooking empanadas and reminded me to soak the raisins before adding them to the filling and to chop the olives up very small.

"We're using frozen pastry, though," I confided, explaining

the morning's failed attempts to make our own from scratch.

I was surprised when she didn't criticize that decision. "Remember when I had you borrow refrigerator biscuits from Juan during dinner rush? We sprinkled on some sesame seeds and no one even noticed."

I did remember, and it made me laugh.

"Everyone is not like us, *cara*," she said. "We're food people. We're a different breed."

Us. I remembered when I'd been part of an us. I remembered belonging. I missed it so much. "Are you all better?" I asked. "Can we go home to Arizona?"

She sighed into the phone. "I am feeling better and hope to visit you soon. But I'm not settled yet," she said. "And you, my Linda, have not yet learned what you need to learn."

"What do you mean?"

"My illness was a factor in my decision to send you to Pat," she said slowly, "but I also feel that you need to learn to live in a family. In your adolescence, you need more than I can give you."

"You mean I can never come home?" My voice rose to a wail.

"Now, Linda. No dramatics. We'll talk about the future another time. For now, I expect you to make this situation work."

Her no-nonsense tone snapped me back into shape, just as it had so many times before. "Okay, Aunt Elba."

"Now, go cook the best empanadas Pittsburgh has ever tasted. And when I feel well enough to visit, I will bring you a little surprise."

I hung up the phone and got busy chopping and soaking and sautéing, and by the time Sir Dad and Chloe came home, the kitchen was flour-free and fragrant.

At least, fragrant to me.

But not to Chloe. "*Ewww!* Are those olives in there?" She wrinkled her nose.

"Yes, olives, and raisins, and cinnamon, and—"

"Please. That's a really weird combination."

I was unwrapping the refrigerated puff pastry. I took a sniff and frowned. "This has Crisco in it."

"How can you tell?"

"I can smell it. Can't you?"

She rolled her eyes. "You and your nose. It smells like nothing to me. Anyway, so what if it *does* have Crisco in it?"

"It's supposed to have butter. Real butter, not margarine. In a pinch, lard."

Chloe shrugged. "Look, we have an hour and a half until we have to start getting ready. Work with it."

"Then get over here and help me." I thrust the rolling pin into her hand and then pulled it away. "I'll roll. You stuff."

We worked away, and even got a lot of semi-decent empanadas folded.

Then the door opened.

In walked Pat, followed by Jen.

"Get out of my kitchen, Linda!" Pat ordered, a furious look on her face. "You're grounded for life, starting with tonight's dance."

"But I—"

"Mom, you can't do that," Chloe said, her voice reasonable. "Linda has to go to the dance. It's a school assignment. Remember we told you about the refreshment committee?"

"Fine. Your punishment starts tomorrow." Pat slammed down her purse on the counter.

What was Pat so upset about? She'd seen me cook before, on Thanksgiving. Okay, I'd broken her rule; but around here, with all of these kids, that happened every day.

I looked at Jen. "What did I do?"

"Check out FabFoodz.com, you little traitor," Jen said.

Chapter Twenty

With a stomach as heavy as a jumbo can of pinto beans, I ran to the computer and logged on to the FabFoodz site.

The moment it came up, there was my page. Featured. The first thing anyone saw when they came to the site.

"Teen Chef Site of the Week!" was the heading.

"Yes!" I whispered, pumping my fist in the air. Most of the teenagers with featured sites were older and in cooking school. I'd never dreamed a newbie fourteen-year-old could get this spot.

But then I looked closer at what was on my page today and crumpled down into the chair, my cheeks on fire.

Because there was the page Pat had seen.

Linda Delgado

<u>CLICK</u> FOR MORE PICTURES

RELATIONSHIP STATUS:

Single

INTERESTS: Food, friends, more food, fun!

How to rescue a horrible dinner made from canned, processed "food":

• Add fresh veggies! Check out my <u>Generic Stuffing with Celery and Onions</u>.

• Add herbs and spices! You can add taste to the blandest macaroni casserole with Mexican spices—take a look at how <u>I jazzed up Bad Beefaroni</u>. Or Barfaroni...

• Give up and start over. Some recipes, like tuna-noodle casserole, just can't be saved.

Friends/Family/Foodie Comments:

Julia says: Wish you'd come over and rescue all the bad dinners at my house, old friend.

Frantic Mom says: Like it! Especially when there's no time to cook fancy.

D. M. says: Italian rules. You should've put basil and oregano in the Beefaroni.

Fresh from Pittsburgh with Trevor and Leslie says: Good try, Linda, but Cooking from Cans is about to drift into the sands of time.

Jen stood behind me, arms crossed. "She saw everything. All the entries making fun of her and the show. You really hurt her, Linda."

"I'll get over it," Pat said from behind us. I turned around. "But I don't know if my show will. All this bad PR is bound to influence the producer." Her voice sounded mechanical, and she didn't meet my eyes.

I tried to say "I'm sorry," but the words got stuck in my throat as Pat left the room.

"I want you out of here," Jen said, her voice low and angry. "You and your little sidekick, Angel." Then she stalked out, too.

I just sat staring at the computer. I had an image of myself now, a true image; and it was as black and sooty as a fire-roasted pepper. What had I done? I'd made horrible, thoughtless comments about a show that, however terrible it was, helped to put food in my mouth. I'd made fun of a woman who'd taken me into her home, had kept me out of foster care. What was wrong with me?

"Come on," Chloe said with a hand on my shoulder. "You've got to get these tarts into the oven, right? And then we have to get dressed. I'll take my shower first while you finish these up."

"But I . . ." I trailed off and walked into the kitchen. How could I explain that I hadn't been thinking of anyone but myself and my own feelings? That I hadn't considered how Pat would feel, hadn't known I would even care about that?

Mechanically, I brushed trays of empanadas with egg white and put them in Pat's industrial-sized oven. Most likely, Pat would kick me out and I'd have to go into foster care. Adjust to a new family in a new part of town. Leave behind Chloe, and Jen, and Sir Dad, and Pat, and all the rest.

I sat there feeling sorry for myself as the empanadas cooked. When the timer went off, I took out the tray.

Without me to help him, Angel would probably go, too, to

another new home where his behavior would get a lot worse and his heart would break a little more.

Tears pushed at the backs of my eyes, so I closed my eyelids and popped a hot empanada into my mouth, hoping to chase away my guilt and my fears. *¡Delicioso!* For just a moment I was back in Arizona, smelling the sage, feeling the hot sun, listening to Spanish. I was home.

But when I swallowed and opened my eyes, I was back in the thick of my Pittsburgh problems.

I hurried through the last two trays, left them out to cool, and rushed upstairs to get ready.

Chloe looked fantastic. For once her preference for black served her well. She'd curled her hair and put in a subtle diamond nose ring that matched her antique-looking faux diamond earrings. She looked feminine and pretty and a little unsure of herself, which was a nice switch from her usual arrogant attitude.

"You look great," I told her. "Dino will totally go for you."

She looked surprised. "Thanks. I hope so." Then she looked me up and down. "Um, you'd better hurry. What are you wearing, anyway?"

At that moment, Jen sailed into our room without knocking. She was holding the ugliest puke-green dress I'd ever laid eyes on. "Here it is," she said, holding it up.

Chloe covered her snort with a cough, but not very well.

"That's . . . the dress . . . you're lending me?" My voice rose into a squeak. "What happened to the red one?"

"Oh, sorry," she said, not sounding sorry at all. "After you tried it on, we didn't hang it back up. The boys came in with some grape Kool-Aid, and the rest is history. The *dress* is history."

"But I look bad in green," I said, holding up the dress to study its lacy front. "Not to mention the fact that I'll never fill this out." I'd had to wear a padded bra with the red dress, but this one didn't have enough fabric to cover a bra. I looked at Jen. "Is this my payback?"

"Part of it," she said, and walked out.

Chloe took the dress from me and studied it doubtfully. "Hurry up and shower, and we'll find a way to stuff the front."

What's the rest of Jen's revenge? I wondered. There was no time to explore it, because getting me ready for the dance was the highest priority.

I had to give Chloe credit: she did her best to help me look decent. By the time I got done with my hair, she'd actually basted bra pads into the dress's halter front. Then she used concealer to cover my zit and lent me some blush and eye makeup to try to counteract the way the green dress turned my complexion putrid.

Despite her efforts, when I looked in the full-length mirror in the hall, I almost cried. "I look like a freak!"

"Well . . . I've seen worse," Chloe said.

"Yeah, at a zombie stroll."

Jen didn't say anything. She just jingled the car keys to let us know she was still driving us to the dance.

All too soon we were pulling up to Dino's house. I wondered what Dino would wear and how he'd act. Even though I felt sick inside about the FabFoodz thing, and even though I knew I was supposed to give him to Chloe, I was excited to spend some time with him.

But when he opened the door and came down the steps, he had company: Nick!

They both slid into the backseat beside Chloe, but with Nick in the middle. I twisted around in the front seat to find Chloe glaring at me. It was like she thought I'd planned this. I shrugged to indicate that it was as much a surprise to me as it obviously was to her, but she looked away very huffily.

My question: was Nick meant for Chloe, or for me?

They gave no clues by their actions. They each talked to both of us.

"Remember, as far as anyone at school knows, I can't cook," Dino said right away. "So no fair telling people that I came to the rescue about the puff pastry."

"Hey," Chloe protested. "You might have had the idea, but Dad and I went out to get it. And Linda mostly made the em-pan-whatevers."

"Yeah," I added, "so don't play like you're some knight in shining armor."

Nick punched at Dino's arm. "Dude, why didn't you help? You're good with pastry."

"Shut up!" Dino punched Nick back. He turned to us and nodded at the tray in his hands. "I do have the cut-up fruit, though."

"Why don't you want anyone to know you can cook?" Jen asked, looking in the rearview mirror. "Girls love that in a guy."

Nick rolled his eyes. "It's the year he spent with those stupid rich relatives, right after his mom died. They looked down on our family business, and now he does, too."

I felt my eyes get wider as I stared at Dino. I hadn't known he'd lost his mother. Something else we had in common.

"So glad I brought you along to tell my life story," Dino said to Nick.

Chloe and I looked at each other, and I felt like we were communicating without words. I had the oddest feeling, like I couldn't wait to be alone with her to hash out this new information.

At least I felt the connection until she opened her mouth. "Well, I can understand why you feel that way," she said to Dino. "My family is totally embarrassing at times, and I hate it when people talk about Mom's cooking show, or about the little United Nations that lives in our house."

Jen pulled up to the school. "Have fun, guys!" she sang out in a suspiciously cheerful voice.

Not. When I stood up and the full glory of my dress was revealed, both Nick and Dino seemed to stare for a minute, then look away. Of course, they ended up looking at Chloe, who was acting unusually animated. "Come on, come on, let's go in," she said, bouncing up and down.

And off they went, leaving me to hunch over the car's hatch and pull out trays of pastry. Naturally, Jen disappeared, too.

I felt sorry for myself even though I knew I deserved it for how I'd mocked Pat on FabFoodz.

Finally, Miss Xavier came to my rescue, bringing a cart from the cafeteria to roll in the empanadas. She helped me set them up on the refreshment table next to the tray of fruit. All the while I was shooting glances around the room, noticing that everyone else seemed to be having a great time. Most people were standing in small clusters, talking to friends. A few were dancing.

Not (thankfully) Dino and Chloe. I didn't see them anywhere.

I snagged an empanada. Still warm, and really tasty. Once everyone realized what great refreshments they had, I told myself, I'd have company and a little recognition over here.

Miss Xavier had my back. When she tasted one of the empanadas, her face broke out into a big smile. "These are marvelous," she said. "Where did you get the recipe?"

"It's a family recipe," I said, feeling proud.

A couple of boys I didn't know came over to check out the food. "What is it?" one of them asked.

"I bet it's, like, McDonald's apple pies," said the other one. He shoved two into his mouth at once before I could warn him that these were savory, not sweet.

He grabbed a napkin and spit them into it. "Ugh. These are awful!"

"They are not. They're delicious," Miss Xavier scolded.

To my surprise, I heard Jen's voice behind me. "If you don't like the nonapple pies, come on over here and try some teeny dogs."

I turned around in time to see her open a pan filled with miniature pigs in a blanket.

"Jen!" I couldn't believe she'd betrayed me like that.

"The choice is yours," she said, smiling everywhere but at me. "These are made with Vienna sausages and canned rolls. They cook up in a flash. Courtesy of Pat's *Cooking from Cans*. Tell your folks."

Mrs. Xavier tried to save me. "Kids, do try one of the empanadas. They're Mexican pastries, and they're quite unusual."

A couple of girls tried my empanadas, but most of the boys gathered around Jen and her tiny dogs, stuffing them into their mouths three at a time. The fruit was fast disappearing, too.

"Linda, where's the rest of the refreshment committee?" asked Miss Xavier.

"Good question," I grouched, looking around. "I'd better go find them."

Little did she know that I had no intention of coming back.

I walked with a purpose until I was out of the sight of Miss Xavier, then slowed down. Maybe I was afraid of what I would find.

Sure enough, there on the dance floor were Chloe and Dino. They looked great, both of them. They were fast dancing; but as I watched, Chloe put her hand on Dino's arm as she laughed at something he was saying, and he grinned and didn't move his arm.

Oh, man. This was what I'd set up to happen; but now that

my plan had gone into action, I felt terrible. I did *not* want them to get together. I just wasn't that self-sacrificing of a person, to give away the boy I really liked.

And I *did* like him, even if he was a little weird, wanting to keep his true background hidden from everyone. In fact, I liked him better now that I understood the reason for his secrets. I wanted to sit down with him and talk about it, to draw him out, to share about how I used to get teased when I came to school smelling of peppers and grease. To talk to him about what it was like to lose your mom.

But now I'd thrown away my chance of that.

As I watched the dance floor, Nick joined Chloe and Dino. All three started kind of dancing together.

Chloe looked ecstatic to be the center of so much attention, and her smile made her whole face glow. If I was a better person, I'd be happy for her. But instead I just felt jealous. I wished I could be the one the boys were admiring.

I heard whispers behind me and turned to see Mindy and Mandy from my cooking class. "Nice dress, Linda," one of them said. They both giggled.

Then I saw Dino walking away from the dance floor. I got a wild hope that he was looking for me, until he veered off toward a group of guy friends. Of course.

Tears rose up into my eyes; and when they started spilling over, I ducked my face and headed for the restroom. This was my lowest low yet. The guy I liked was sparking for my cousin. Pat, Jen, and Chloe were all against me. I was probably going to lose even these people, who were at least familiar, and have to start over again somewhere else. And I couldn't get any comfort from cooking, because everyone in the city—except some middle-aged teacher—hated my food.

I'd really tried to make it here in Pittsburgh. Tried to make it in a family, like Aunt Elba wanted me to.

And I'd failed.

I had to do something. Ignoring the curious stares and giggles of the girls' bathroom crowd, I wiped away my smeared makeup and adjusted my sagging bra pads. I pulled my hair up off my sweaty neck into a knot.

I'd still have to stop at home and change my clothes; but as soon as I did that and found the bus schedule online, I was running away.

Running home. Home to empanada country. Maybe Julia's family could take me in.

I marched out of the bathroom and into the school hallway, thinking.

Julia's family didn't have a big place, but I wouldn't be any more crowded with them than I was at Pat's house. And I'd much rather have Julia for a roommate than Chloe.

Wouldn't I?

I leaned back against the wall biting my lip as a movie of images intruded on my dream of going back home. Chloe, helping me conceal my zit and fix up my dress for the dance. Pat, rushing in from the studio to cook a huge, if bad, dinner for us every single night. Jen, acting upbeat even when she didn't feel that way inside. Angel, being his own crazy, lovable self.

What should I do? Should I stay or should I go?

While I was pondering, Dino walked out of the gym. "Where have you been?" he asked. "I've been looking for you."

"I got a little discouraged about . . . things."

He looked at me hard. "It's the food, isn't it?"

"That, and other stuff."

"C'mere. We can fix it." He pulled me into the gym and over to the refreshment table. "Hey, guys," Dino called to everyone standing nearby. "Anyone like frozen pizza rolls? Or frozen egg rolls?"

A bunch of people said they did.

"Well, these are like that, only Mexican. They're great!"

He popped an empanada into his mouth, chewed it slowly, and smiled his sexy smile.

Immediately, there was a run on the empanada table—mostly girls, of course.

While they tasted the empanadas, Dino charmed them by telling them they looked good in their dresses, or teasing them about their boyfriends, or sympathizing with their diet goals that my empanadas were sabotaging.

And after the crowd thinned out, he stood there eating empanadas and smiling at me.

Flustered, I looked around and saw Chloe deep in conversation with Nick. And she was sort of smiling instead of biting his head off.

When I turned back, Dino dusted off his hands on a napkin and came over to stand beside me.

A little closer than just friends.

"Why'd you stand up for me about the empanadas?" I asked him. "Someone might guess you have a cooking background."

He leaned in even closer. "Believe it or not, I do listen to you."

My stomach fluttered. "No kidding?"

"No kidding. Like I said the other day, I realized I do have more fun in the Strip than I do at school." He shrugged. "Besides, I'm starting to think that cooking can be way cool."

"Oh, yeah?"

"When you do it, yeah."

So that was nice.

And when he held out his arms to dance with me, that was even nicer. For once I could linger in how good he smelled, and tell him about it, and feel his arms—strong from cooking—

around me. At one point I caught Chloe looking at us, and she gave me an eye roll. But she was talking to Nick, and didn't really look as upset as I'd expected.

I still wasn't feeling quite right inside, though. I kept thinking about Pat. And about how sad and discouraged I feel when people don't like my cooking—that was what she must be feeling on a larger scale.

And maybe she'd kick me out for it. But even if she took the high road and let me stay—which, knowing Pat, was likely—she was still upset, and her show was on the rocks.

I didn't know how to fix all that; but like Aunt Elba always says, when in doubt, take action.

And because of who I am, I suddenly knew exactly what kind of action I wanted to take. So I allowed myself one more dance in Dino's arms; and then I got him and Chloe and Nick, and we called Jen, and we all went to work.

Chapter Twenty-one

"I'm not so sure about this," Chloe said as we hauled our clanking grocery bags into Dino's house.

Nick wrapped his hands around her throat from behind in a fake choke hold. "No negativity," he growled.

Chloe giggled, a sound I'd rarely heard. Then Jen tripped on the doorstep and stumbled into me, and we fell into a heap in the tiled entryway, cans clattering around us. I tried to stifle my laughter. Jen didn't.

"*Sssh!* My dad's a light sleeper," Dino warned.

Too late.

Heavy footsteps crossed the floor upstairs as we tried to collect the spilled cans. Before we could finish, Mr. Moretti stumped down the stairs, a sight to behold in his green plaid pajamas, with his hair sticking out at wild angles.

I heard Jen choke back another giggle. But he was just scary enough so that none of us laughed out loud.

"What are you crazy kids doing?" he asked in a voice that was irritated and rough with sleep.

I wondered whether Aunt Pat would have the same reaction. "Dad, it's okay," Dino said.

I couldn't leave him hanging there to explain alone. "It was my idea, sir," I said, stepping forward. I cleared my throat. "I did something that really upset Aunt Pat, and I figured a party with a lot of her kind of food was the way to make it up to her. I talked these guys into helping me."

"And I said we could do the cooking here." Dino's voice was steady and confident. "Because you'd understand how food can fix problems."

Mr. Moretti glared at us for a moment more, then sighed, sat down on the stairs, and rubbed his eyes. "Do you know what time it is?"

"Yeah. It's . . ."—Nick pulled out his phone to check—"eleven thirty."

"And do you know how much of a mess it will make, cooking all of this . . ." He trailed off, staring at the can-filled bags. "What in the name of Saint Martha are you cooking?"

"We're cooking everything from cans," I admitted, feeling a little ashamed. "Because it's what Aunt Pat believes in, and I was mean to make fun of it."

"It'll be good. You'll see." Jen gave him a winning smile. "And we'll clean up the mess."

"And your parents, do they know where you are?"

"We stopped at our house to change and explained everything to my dad." Even though Chloe was back to her usual goth appearance, she sounded respectful and responsible. "We have permission."

Luckily, Pat had been asleep when we'd stopped by. And hopefully, Sir Dad had come up with a story that Pat—if she woke up—would believe about where we were.

Mr. Moretti propped his cheek on his hand and looked at us. Then he seemed to make a decision. "All right. Nick. Dino.

Front and center." He gestured for them to come to the front of the stairs.

They looked at each other and did what he said.

"You do this. It is a worthy plan. But cook something good. Show your heritage!"

"Sure, Dad," Dino said.

Nick saluted. "Will do, sir!"

Jen reached over and squeezed my hand. We were in!

At one point when I was bending over to pick up some heavy cans, I turned around to see Dino ogling me from behind.

"Hey, get up here and help," I said, my cheeks heating.

"But the view's so good back here!"

That led to a little scuffle in which he wrestled me against the counter. His hands circled my wrists and his broad chest was just an inch away from me. I smelled the woodsy soap he used.

All of a sudden I was having that spicy feeling again, kind of breathless, like I'd eaten too many extrahot peppers all at once. I met his eyes, which turned serious, and I thought he might kiss me . . . but over his shoulder, I saw Chloe looking at us. I turned away and got very busy opening cans.

When I had the chance, I pulled Chloe into the pantry. "Look, I'm sorry about Dino," I said. "I really did mean for him to get together with you at the dance. And for a while, I thought it was happening."

"It was never happening," she said, rolling her eyes. "He likes you better."

"Ummm . . ." I couldn't deny that it seemed to be true, though I wasn't confident enough to believe it completely.

"You don't have to pretend otherwise. He's nuts about you. It's obvious. You should have kissed him back there."

My jaw about dropped. "You're not mad about it?"

"I'm not thrilled, but I have to accept reality. He talked about you the whole time we were dancing tonight. And I'm not going to be evil about it when you're doing all this for Mom."

Impulsively, I reached out and hugged her. "Thanks, Chloe."

She twisted away. "Hey, hey, hey. Enough of that." As we walked back out into the kitchen, she poked a small hole in my happy balloon. "You know, Mom doesn't like surprises. She may hate this."

"How can she hate it when we're cooking all of her awful food?"

"Food snob, " Jen accused.

I looked to Dino and Nick for support, but they were busy consulting over a cookbook.

I turned back to Jen and Chloe. "I admit it: I am a food snob. But I mean, look at this." I gestured at the recycling bin filled entirely with our empty cans. "It's an ecological nightmare. Your mom should love it."

"You may have noticed," Jen said, "that Mom is a teeny bit controlling."

"Especially where food is concerned," Chloe added.

They were right. Was I crazy, trying to help Pat by cooking from cans? Was all of this going to backfire?

But there was no point in changing my mind now. I'd committed every penny I had to this, and the food was bought. "Come on, let's get busy," I said, and we did.

Even though we were cooking truly bizarre food, we had a lot of fun doing it. We turned some music on low, and the smell of tomato sauce and frying meat filled the air. I was back in the kitchen with fun people I cared about, and that was more important than how fresh the ingredients were. But I did have to smile when I noticed Nick and Dino chopping fresh garlic and basil to spice up their manicotti.

Chloe noticed, too, and poked an accusatory finger at them. "That's not how Mom makes Italian food," she said.

Nick reached out, grabbed her finger, and pulled her toward him. "Just smell," he coaxed. "It's good. It's the food of love."

Jen and I giggled. I was expecting Chloe to punch him out. But to my surprise she leaned over the baking dish, inhaled, and smiled. "You *do* have a way with spices," she said in a throaty voice.

"That's not all I have a way with," he said close to her ear in a voice I could barely hear.

She playfully slapped him. Very un-Chloe. But I didn't have time to analyze the moment.

"Do you think this is going to work?" I asked Jen as we dumped an industrial-sized can of mandarin oranges into the five-cup salad. "Or do you really think Pat will hate it?"

"Who knows," she said. "But she couldn't get much more miserable than she was after the whole FabFoodz episode today."

"Guilty as charged," I said miserably. "I was a jerk."

"Yep! You were. But you're a doll for trying to fix it, and maybe she'll see it that way, too." Jen smiled at me.

"Or maybe not," Chloe said behind us in her ever-helpful way.

Chapter Twenty-two

"*Sssh!* She's coming!" Jen gestured for everyone to take their appointed places.

I couldn't resist peeking out the window. Pat was struggling out of the car, pulling her heavy satchel from work.

My stomach tightened as I looked around the room, wondering if I'd made a huge mistake in setting up all this. We'd cooked late into the night at Dino's house, then stumbled home to bed for just a few hours. As soon as Pat had left for the studio this morning, we'd started calling friends and cleaning the house.

We'd even decorated, sort of. Arching across the kitchen doorway was a giant banner: CHRISTMAS FROM CANS!

The dining-room table was laden with foods I'd never thought I would feel proud to serve: cranberry Jell-O fluff, baked ham with canned pineapple, chicken-stuffing casserole, manicotti, baked bean salad with mayonnaise, wiener-and-creamed corn mix-up.

And the room was full of people: all the kids in the family, Sir Dad, Mrs. Piotrowski and her hockey-loving boyfriend, Dino and his dad, Nick, and a bunch of other friends from church and the neighborhood. Jen had sweet-talked one of her boyfriends into bringing a high-quality video camera, so the whole event could be streamed live to my FabFoodz site. We'd even invited the producer of *Cooking from Cans*, though he hadn't shown up.

"*Ssssh!*" All eyes were fixed on the front door.

Pat opened it and walked in.

"Surprise!" everyone yelled.

I had a moment of terror: could shock make you miscarry?

But Pat didn't look like she was going to have a medical emergency; she looked like she was going to have a psychological one. "What's going on here?"

Everyone looked at me.

"It was Linda's idea," Sam said quickly. "I didn't want to do it."

"Go ahead and explain," Sir Dad prompted me, walking forward to put an arm around Pat.

"I, uh, we wanted to do something to make you feel better," I said. "It's all from cans," I added quickly.

She drew in a deep breath as if she was about to yell at me. Then she took another look at the room, at the people watching her, their faces anxious, and pulled out her television personality. "Well, isn't this the craziest thing," she said. "Thank you all! It's so sweet of you!" And she walked up to the table and started admiring the food.

Everyone relaxed and started talking, but I could tell she wasn't thrilled. What was wrong? Was it because I hadn't asked permission? Because we'd added in some fresh garlic and onions here and there? Because Dino and Nick had cooked up a version of baked manicotti that wasn't entirely from cans?

As soon as I could, I pulled her away from all the people. In a corner of the living room, I turned to her. "I'm really sorry, Pat. I did it without asking you, and I guess I shouldn't have."

She gave me a resigned half smile. "Yes, I'd have preferred for you to get permission from me, but what's done is done."

"There's something else I want to talk to you about," I went on, speaking quickly so I wouldn't lose my courage. "Pat, I am so sorry for what I said about your show on the FabFoodz site. I was wrong to make fun of you. It was mean of me. That's why I wanted to make you a party. To apologize."

I stood waiting for her to kick me out right then and there. But instead she gave me a hug. "Oh, Linda, after all this time being a mother, I know that kids have to be kids, and teenagers have to rebel." She grabbed a tissue and blew her nose. "It's sweet that you did this for me. Really, it is. But the show is a bust. I haven't been able to stop thinking about it, and I could b-b-barely film today."

I handed her another tissue. "No, it's not! You can come back. We're getting this party on film and streaming it to my FabFoodz page. And we'll stream it to yours if it's okay with you, and we invited your producer—"

She shook her head. "You've been right all along. I just didn't want to accept it. Beyond our family, beyond a few frazzled Midwestern moms, beyond Pittsburgh, canned food is history. Everything's going organic; everything's fresh. The show is a goner, and I finally realize that."

Chloe came rushing over and interrupted our blubbery chat. "Good news and bad news," she said breathlessly. "The good news is: this party's for you, Mom! Come enjoy it!"

Pat and I gawked at Chloe's unusually animated attitude. "What's the bad news?" Pat asked.

"Well, Trevor, Leslie, and their kid just showed up."

I couldn't believe it. "Who invited them?"

"No one. I think they saw the live feed on FabFoodz."

"They're crashing our party?"

"Yeah, and Jen's trying to keep them under control, but it's not exactly working."

"What should we do?"

Chloe shrugged. "This is your show, Linda."

It *was* my show.

I marched over to where Trevor and Leslie stood surveying the scene. "Hi, guys," I said, putting on a cheerful voice. "The more, the merrier around here! Come on in and have some food. It's all from cans."

"I don't quite get it," Trevor said in a whiny voice. "What's the occasion? Is Channel Eight doing some special promotion for Pat, and we weren't informed?"

"No, we're just having a party," I said.

"Yeah," Jen chimed in behind me. "Let me help you to some green bean casserole."

"You know," Trevor said, "my mother used to make that."

"Everybody's mother did." Leslie wrinkled her nose. "That doesn't make it good."

"Well . . . I guess there's a certain nostalgia value," Trevor said, clearly trying to be more polite than his wife.

Nostalgia value? Was that all Pat's show had to offer? I didn't know what to say.

Chloe came to the rescue. "Excuse me, but this isn't nostalgia. This is real life for us."

"And for a lot of other families, too," Jen chimed in. "Here. Fill a plate."

Trevor and Leslie joined everyone else digging into the food. Predictably, though, they acted all offended by the tastes and smells, and I was reminded of how I'd reacted to the food when I'd first come to town. Seeing someone else do it made me realize how snotty and babyish I'd been.

Suddenly, Leslie's eyebrows shot up. "Wait a minute. Is this really canned?" She held up a forkful of baked manicotti.

I looked over at Dino and Nick. "Is it?"

"Yeah, mostly," Nick said easily. "We used canned tomatoes

but fresh spices. So I guess it's a compromise."

Compromise. There was that word again.

Just then Samantha came out from behind her video game and poked at her mother. "I'm hungry," she whined.

"Don't eat any of this food," Leslie said quickly. "I've got some veggie chips in my bag." She gave us a smirky smile. "She won't eat anything nonorganic."

"*Sí,* she will." Angel turned from his LEGO project. "She steals my lunch almost every day."

"Angel! You promised you wouldn't tell!" The foodie princess herself ran over and whacked him in the face.

"Samantha!" Leslie's face went red. At first I thought she was mad that her daughter had hit another child. *Not.* "I can't believe you would steal whatever processed junk that woman packs for him. The very idea!"

"Almost every day. She doesn't like veggie chips and brown bread. We sometimes trade but . . ." Angel shrugged. "Usually we share, and her lunch ends up in the garbage."

"Now, don't feel bad," Mrs. Piotrowski said to Leslie. "My children didn't like homemade food when they were small, either. Why, they'd rather have a Twinkie than a Polish pastry any day."

It felt like we were on the verge of a revelation when the doorbell rang, interrupting everything. Who was it now? Mindy and Mandy?

But when I opened the door, a wonderful, familiar, spicy smell hit me. "Aunt Elba?" I asked, unable to believe my eyes.

She held out her arms, and I practically jumped into them. Then I helped her inside with her suitcases and took her coat as she straightened her sweater and patted her hair back into place. "Did I hurt you? Are you okay?" I asked her.

"I'm as good as new—almost." She waved away her taxi,

then turned to me with a big smile. I could see that she'd lost a few pounds and her neck wasn't blotchy.

"Why are you here?" All of a sudden, fear filled me. "Did Aunt Pat ask you to come get me? Do I have to go into foster care?"

"No, no, no. Late last night your cousins Jen and Chloe let me know about the party, and I was able to get a last-minute deal on a flight." She stroked my cheek. "I was really happy to hear that you were doing something nice for Pat."

When we came into the living room, there was a wave of excited introductions. Everyone hurried to make Aunt Elba feel welcome: Jen brought her a plate of food, and the boys moved their action figures out of her way, and Chloe led her to a prime spot by the fire.

Trevor and Leslie obviously didn't like being out of the spotlight, and they left, dragging a sobbing Samantha with them. "But nobody ever comes to our house," she wailed as they headed out the door. "I like it here."

Some of the kids settled down to play Sir Dad's favorite game, Star Wars Monopoly, and the rest of the adults joined Aunt Elba in front of the fire.

"I have something for you," Aunt Elba told me, reaching into her giant satchel. She pulled out a red, leather-bound book.

There, on laminated pages, were all of the family recipes! The yellowed ones, with beautiful drawings, for empanadas, and ranchero sauce, and sweet rice.

"You're giving your recipes to me?" I gasped when I realized what the book contained. "But don't you need . . . you're not . . ." I didn't want to say my thoughts out loud. Was this her way of telling me she was going to die?

"No, no," she said, reading my mind. "You need them now. For me the recipes are all up here." She tapped her temple. "It is time for you to have them. And in your day, you will pass them on to your own daughter."

"Thank you," I said, choking back tears. I leaned my head against her knee like I was five years old again, paging through the precious cookbook. "I'll take good care of it."

"And *use* it. That is most important."

"I will," I promised.

Chloe, Jen, and I kept everyone's plates and drink glasses full, and brainstormed about how great it would be if *Cooking from Cans* went national until Pat held up her hand. "Girls," she said, "I appreciate what you're doing, but I can't keep beating a dead horse. We all know there's some good and easy food you can cook from cans, but let's face it: it's hopelessly old-fashioned. Most of the country wants fresh food these days."

"It's true. Community gardens are the new fad in Texas," Aunt Elba said.

"I just don't want Trevor and Leslie to be right," Jen said. "They're so snooty. Who wants to watch them on TV?"

"Old-fashioned is bad, but retro is cool," Chloe observed.

I butted into the conversation. "What about a compromise?" I asked, using my favorite new word. "Can't people do what Dino and Nick did? Use some canned food and some fresh, and make stuff that's easy, that works for busy people, but that has some . . ." I trailed off, not wanting to insult Pat.

"Some pizzazz?" she supplied, raising her eyebrows at me.

I grinned. "Yeah."

"I like *Mamá* Pat's cooking," Angel said. That was when I noticed he wasn't playing with the other kids but was instead huddled by the fireplace. He wasn't looking at Pat, though. He was watching Aunt Elba.

"It's important," Mrs. Piotrowski said, "to cook food that children will like. And your children do like your cooking, Pat.

For the most part." She glanced at me, a smile dancing around the corners of her mouth.

"You can add pizzazz with ethnic food," Aunt Elba suggested. "Spices from Mexico add a lot of flavor."

"Yes, they do. As do spices from Poland," Mrs. P added.

"So maybe you should pitch it to the network: *Canned with Pizzazz*," I said.

Pat shrugged. "There are possibilities," she said. "People like the warmth of my show; and if we can modernize it, maybe we can capture a bigger slice of the audience. A retro show with a modern touch. It's worth a try."

Aunt Elba gave me an approving pat on the arm.

I felt like a huge weight had come off me; and it was even better when Jen, Chloe, Dino, and Nick pulled me out into the kitchen for a group hug.

"We did it! We threw the best party ever!" Jen was jumping up and down.

"And we brought Mom back from the abyss," Chloe added.

"*Cooking from Cans* rules!" That was me, and then I slapped myself on the side of the head. "Who'd have ever thought I would say that?"

Dino wrapped his arms around me from behind. "Anyone who knew you," he said. "They'd know you'd stand up for the people you love and the things you believe in. And I, for one, think that's pretty cool."

I leaned back and basked in the warmth of his arms and the delicious, spicy scent of him. *Yum!*

A little later, I went over to the fireplace again. Aunt Elba and Pat were the only ones left there—oh, and Angel, who was nearly asleep in Aunt Elba's lap. They were talking lazily about the new show idea, the coming baby, and relatives they'd known long ago.

Pat was looking thoughtful. "I would definitely appreciate consulting with you on the show," she told Aunt Elba, "if and when you move up this way. Making it more ethnic—that's not something I know a whole lot about."

Miracles, miracles. Pat admitted she didn't know everything.

"I can help you even while I stay in Texas," Aunt Elba said, surprising me. "Linda can show us how to use the computer to consult, yes? It's time I get with the modern age, too."

I held my breath. Did that mean Aunt Elba wanted me to come back to Texas with her? Or stay here? "Where would I show you how to use the computer? Here?"

"In Texas," Aunt Elba said, smiling. "Now that I'm feeling better and Pat's baby is coming, I've been thinking you should come back with me."

"I could really use Linda here now," Pat cut in.

I looked from one to the other. "You both want me?"

"She may want you, but I *need* you," Pat said. "With the new baby coming and Jen leaving for college, I'll need some help with cooking. And . . ."—she gave me a rueful smile—"I could maybe even use an in-house consultant for revamping the show."

Aunt Elba reached out to stroke my arm. "It's your choice, Linda. You've learned what you needed to learn." She paused. "Although, considering my parents, Pat's home may be the friendlier place to live."

"What about Angel?" I asked Pat. "If I stay, can he? Is there room for both of us?"

Pat rubbed a hand across her face. "Looking at him now, so peaceful, I'd say that of course there's room. We've made it this far. And for the first six months or so, the new baby will sleep in our room."

"And maybe by then I'll be well enough to move closer and help you more," Aunt Elba said, stroking Angel's hair.

I took a deep breath and blew it out, and looked around the room. All of a sudden I knew: this crazy place was home, and these were my people. I was needed here.

So, for now, I would stay.

And with that decision, love—swirling all around me like the aroma of freshly baked *pan dulce*—poured into that dark, empty place inside me, filling me all the way up, at last.

Linda Delgado

CLICK FOR MORE PICTURES

RELATIONSHIP STATUS:

Single

INTERESTS: Food, friends, more food, fun!

What I'm cooking today: Breakfast, lunch, and dinner for eleven—my aunt Elba is staying for two more days.

What else I'm doing: Enjoying my family!

Friends/Family/Foodie Comments:

Julia says: I can't wait to see you—so glad your aunt is paying for my visit over break!

Linda says: Aunt Pat is generous. Visit her website, everybody, at CookingFromCans.com to find out about her new, revamped show.

Hank says: I love you! When can I meet you?

Dino says: You can't, dude. She's taken.

Linda says: Food equals love. Eat!

Full Recipe for Aunt Elba's Empanadas

Empanada Dough:

3 cups flour
½ teaspoon salt
1½ sticks cold, firm butter, chopped into pieces
1 egg
1 tablespoon vinegar
a few tablespoons water

Combine flour and salt. Cut in butter using two knives. (There's a YouTube video to see how this is done if you don't have an Aunt Elba in your life!) Then knead in egg, vinegar, and a couple tablespoons of water, more if needed, to make a dough. As soon as it's a lump, a little drier than store-bought cookie dough, stop!

If you're not rushing to get these ready for a school dance, let the dough chill in the fridge for a half hour. Then roll out the dough until it's about ¼ inch thick. (Aunt Elba can get it as thin as ⅛ inch, but she's a genius.)

Use a standard-sized coffee can to cut the dough into circles. You're ready for the next step!

Empanada Filling:

1 onion, chopped small
1–2 cloves fresh minced garlic
1 tsp. olive oil
pinch chile powder
1 sweet pepper, red or green, chopped small
1 pound ground beef

3 tablespoons raisins, soaked in warm water until softened, then drained
3 tablespoons chopped olives
3 chopped tomatoes, fresh, of course!
egg white or melted butter for coating (optional)

Sauté onion and garlic in olive oil. Add pepper. When tender, set aside.

In the same pan, fry ground beef until it's no longer pink and drain if it's fatty. Then add raisins, olives, tomatoes, chile powder, and the pepper and onions, and let it cook ten minutes or so.

Make the Empanadas:

Preheat oven to 350F°. Put a spoonful of filling onto half of each dough circle. Moisten the edges, then fold the circles over so that they're like little half-moon pillows, and press the edges closed with a fork. Brush with egg white if you want them shiny or with melted butter if you want them extra tasty!

Bake for 15–20 minutes, until golden brown.

¡Delicioso!